They were both masked and they could pretend...

God, she needed to pretend.

"Kiss me."

Cal couldn't see Quinn's expression beneath his mask, and it was too dark to see the emotion in his eyes. She felt his hesitation and worried that he would back off, that he'd yank them back to reality, to their lives. When his mouth softened, she knew that he was as tempted as she was.

He finally ducked his head and his mouth hovered over hers, teasing.

Minutes, hours, eons later, he lowered his head and his mouth brushed hers. His fingertips dug into the bare skin at her waist, and by their own volition her hands parted his jacket to touch the muscles at his waist, to echo his hold on her.

As he kissed her, as she lost herself in him, the world faded away, melting in the joy his mouth created. In this moment, as his mouth invaded hers, she wasn't the good girl, the do-gooder with the sterling reputation.

She was Cal, and Quinn holding her was all that was important.

* * *

Married to the Maverick Millionaire is part of the From Mavericks to Married series—Three superfine hockey players finally meet their matches!

Dear Reader,

Quinn Rayne is running out of friends to play with. Kade and Mac have both fallen in love, but the biggest Maverick playboy is not prepared to give up his hard-living, fast-paced and adrenaline-filled lifestyle to settle down. However, Quinn's bad-boy behavior has caught up with him, and he is no longer the Maverick darling. The press, Maverick fans and, most important, the Maverick's business partner are all tired of Quinn's antics and have decided that it's time for the Maverick's coach to settle down.

His oldest and best friend, heiress Callahan Adam-Carter, has been married once and that was a disaster, so she, like Quinn, is content with her single lifestyle. When Cal returns to Vancouver, her dead husband's lawyer informs her that, since she has not remarried five years after his death, she is due to inherit a ridiculous amount of money from his estate. Cal doesn't want or need his money, and that means she has to marry...and quickly.

Cal sees a way to kill two pesky birds with one stone. She's the city's favorite daughter, and by marrying her, Quinn can rehabilitate his reputation and Cal can avoid inheriting Toby Carter's tainted money. She and Quinn are friends, best friends. After a year or so they'll divorce and they'll still be friends. What could possibly go wrong? *cue evil author cackling*

Kade, Mac and Quinn are three of my favorite characters, and I hope you enjoy spending time with them—I've loved every minute.

Happy reading!

Joss

Connect with me at www.josswoodbooks.com

Twitter: @josswoodbooks

Facebook: Joss Wood Author

JOSS WOOD

MARRIED TO THE
MAVERICK MILLIONAIRE

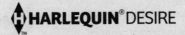

Recycling programs
for this product may
not exist in your area.

ISBN-13: 978-0-373-73503-7

Married to the Maverick Millionaire

Copyright © 2016 by Joss Wood

This edition published by arrangement with Harlequin Books S.A.

For questions and comments about the quality of this book, please contact us at CustomerService@Harlequin.com.

Printed in U.S.A.

www.Harlequin.com

Joss Wood's passion for putting black letters on a white screen is matched only by her love of books and traveling (especially to the wild places of southern Africa) and, possibly, by her hatred of ironing and making school lunches.

Joss has written over sixteen books for the Harlequin KISS, Harlequin Presents and, most recently, Harlequin Desire lines.

After a career in business lobbying and local economic development, Joss now writes full-time. She lives in KwaZulu-Natal, South Africa, with her husband and two teenage children, surrounded by family, friends, animals and a ridiculous amount of books.

Joss is a member of the RWA (Romance Writers of America) and ROSA (Romance Writers of South Africa).

Books by Joss Wood

Harlequin Desire

Taking the Boss to Bed

From Mavericks to Married

Trapped with the Maverick Millionaire
Pregnant by the Maverick Millionaire
Married to the Maverick Millionaire

Harlequin Presents

One Night, Two Consequences
Her Boss by Day...
Behind the Headlines

Visit her Author Profile page at Harlequin.com, or josswoodbooks.com, for more titles.

This book is dedicated to my own Cal,
the port I run to in any storm.
I am so grateful to have you in my life.

One

Quinn Rayne flew across the parking lot on the Coal Harbour promenade, his feet slapping an easy but fast rhythm as he dodged both tourists and residents taking a late afternoon stroll on the paved and pretty walking and biking path next to the marina. The earbuds in his ears and his dark sunglasses were an excellent excuse to ignore the calls of recognition, the pointed fingers.

Even after a decade of being in the spotlight, he still wasn't used to being an object of curious, sometimes disapproving, fascination. Surely the residents of Vancouver could find someone new to discuss? There had to be someone in the city who was a bigger badass than he was reputed to be.

As he approached the marina, he slowed his sprint

to a jog and then to a walk, fingers against the pulse point in his neck and his eyes on his watch. After two minutes he nodded, satisfied. He might not be playing professional ice hockey anymore, but he was as fit as he'd ever been. He'd see whether his players, when they returned to practice next week, had also maintained their fitness. For their sakes, he hoped so.

Quinn walked to the access gate to his wharf. He punched in his code to open the gate and jogged down to where his yacht was berthed. Because he owned one of the prime sites, he had unobstructed views of Burrard Inlet, with Stanley Park to his left and Grouse Mountain in front of him. Living on the water was more adventurous than living in a house and God knew how much he craved adventure.

Quinn stepped onto the *Red Delicious* and quickly ran up the steps to the main deck, the quickest way to access the living area. He slid open the door, pulled his earbuds from his neck and tossed them, his cap and his sunglasses onto the sleek table to his right. He glanced at his watch and wondered if he had time for a shower before Mac and Kade arrived to report back on a meeting they'd attended earlier with Warren Bayliss, their partner and investor.

Bayliss was an essential part of the ongoing process to buy the Mavericks franchise from the current owner, Myra Hasselback, who was also considering selling out to a Russian billionaire who owned a string of boring sports franchises. Quinn didn't need his brother's string of degrees to know that when he, a full Mavericks partner, was excluded from the meeting Warren called, then there was trouble in paradise.

And that it had his name on it.

Quinn walked into the massive open-plan living area and immediately noticed the small form tucked into the corner of his oversized sofa, a cup of coffee in her hand, staring out of the floor-to-ceiling glass windows. One foot was tucked up under her butt; her other—long, slim and sexy—was bent. She'd been sitting like that on the beach at Sandy Cove the first day he'd met her, gap-toothed and grinning, a six-year-old dynamo. She was his girl-next-door or, to be technical, the girl from three houses down. His childhood companion and his teenage confidante.

Sensing his presence, she turned her head, deep-red curls bouncing. Freckles splattered across her nose and onto her cheeks, each one perfect. God, he loved her freckles, had missed those freckles, her face.

He slapped his hands on his hips, not sure if he was just imagining her or if she was really sitting there, bright hair and makeup-free but so damn real he could barely breathe.

"*Red.* What the hell are you doing here?"

Her smile slammed into his sternum and Quinn's heart bounced off his rib cage. Callahan's deep, dark eyes danced as she jumped to her feet and Quinn found himself smiling, properly smiling, for the first time that day. He reached out, grabbed her and swept her into his arms. She weighed less than a feather and he easily whirled her around. The scent of wildflowers hovered around her. It was in the hair he buried his face into, on the warm, smooth skin he could feel beneath the barrier of her shirt. Her laugh rumbled through her and instantly lightened his mood. She'd always had the naughtiest, dirtiest laugh.

Cal Adam was back and his world made a little more sense.

Her feet still off the ground, Cal placed her hands on his shoulders and pushed away from him, her eyes clashing with his. "Hi."

"Hi back."

"You always had the prettiest eyes," Cal said, the tips of her fingers coming to rest on his cheekbone. "Ice green with a ring of emerald." She patted his cheek and rubbed her hand through his too-long, overly full beard. "Not sure about this, though. You're hiding that sexy face."

Quinn tightened his arms, his lower body responding as she wound her legs around his waist. A picture of her wet and naked, in exactly this position, appeared on his internal big screen, but he brushed it away. This was Cal, his oldest friend, his best friend—having lascivious thoughts about her was weird. And wrong.

He patted her small, tight butt. "Glad to see that you've picked up a bit of weight since the last time I saw you." It had been nearly two years ago and she'd been in hospital with a stomach bug she'd caught in Panama.

Cal had looked almost skeletal. Always petite, at least she now looked on the healthy side of slim.

Cal smiled again, dropped a quick kiss on his lips, a kiss that had Quinn wanting more, needing to find out whether her lips were as soft as they appeared, whether that mouth that looked like it had been made for sin could, actually, sin. What was his problem? Was he now such a player that it was a habit to take every encounter with every woman to the bedroom? Even Cal?

Cal wiggled, her feet dropped to the maple floor and Quinn released her. She stepped back and pushed a curl behind her ear.

"*Red Delicious*, Q? That's an odd name for a boat." Cal made a production of fluttering her eyelashes. "Or did you name it after me?"

He grinned. "You wish I did. Nope, it was pure co-incidence."

"Honestly, she's stunning," Cal stated, looking around. Quinn followed her gaze. The sleek lines of the sixty-five-meter yacht were echoed in the minimalist furniture and cool white, grey and beige. Sometimes he thought it a little stark...

"It needs some color. Some bold prints, some bright cushions," Cal said, echoing his thoughts. Despite their long time apart, they still thought along the same lines.

"She's beautiful and bigger than your last yacht. How many does she sleep?"

"Ten on the lower deck. The master cabin is aft with

a walk-in wardrobe and spa bath and there's another full cabin forward. Two small cabins midship There's another smaller, cozier lounge…that's where I watch TV, wind down. Two decks, one off the main bedroom and another entertainment deck with a Jacuzzi."

"Impressive. I want to see it all. When did you acquire her?"

"About a year back." Quinn ran a hand down Cal's hair and her curls wound around his knuckle. The smell of her shampoo wafted over to him and he wondered when Cal's hair had turned so soft and silky. So damned girly. Cal shoved her hands into the back pockets of her skinny jeans and arched her back. The white silk T-shirt pulled against her chest and Quinn noticed her small, perky breasts and that she was wearing a lacy, barely-there push-up bra.

He rolled his shoulders, uncomfortable. *Right. Enough with that, Rayne.*

Quinn rubbed the back of his neck as he walked across the living area to the kitchen. He opened the double-door fridge and peered inside, hoping that the icy air would cool his lascivious thoughts.

"Water?" he asked, his words muffled.

Cal shook her head. "No, thanks."

He slammed the fridge door closed and cracked the lid on the water bottle before lifting it to his lips.

"How is your dad?" he asked, remembering why she was back in the city, back home.

"Okay. The triple heart bypass was successful. I went

straight from the airport to the hospital and spent some time with him. He was awake and making plans so I suppose that's a good sign."

"I'm glad he's okay."

"He'll be fine. Stressing about when he can get back to work." He saw the worry in her eyes, heard fear in her flat tone. "The doctors said he won't be able to return to work for a couple of months and that sent him into a tailspin."

"He had the operation a few days ago. Maybe he should relax a little. The foundation won't grind to a stop because he isn't there."

The Adam Foundation was the wealthiest charitable organization in Canada, funded by the accumulated wealth of generations of her Adam ancestors. Money from the Adam Foundation allowed an ever-changing group of volunteers, and Cal, to travel the world to assist communities who needed grassroots help.

Cal bit the inside of her lip and her arched eyebrows pulled together. "He'll need somebody to run it until he's back on his feet."

"Is that person you?" he asked, annoyed by the spurt of excitement he felt. God, he and Cal hadn't lived in the same city for ages and having her around would be a very nice change.

"Maybe," Cal replied, unenthusiastic. "We'll talk about it later."

Quinn frowned as he tried to work out why Cal felt so ambivalent toward the city they'd been raised in. It was beautiful, interesting and eclectic, but Cal only came home when she absolutely had to. Maybe it had something to do with the fact that her husband had been killed when the light aircraft he'd been piloting crashed into a mountain to the north of the city around four... no, it had to be five years ago now.

She'd married the same week she turned twenty-four and, thanks to their massive argument about her nuptials—Quinn had loudly and vociferously told her that she'd lost her mind—he'd missed both her birthday and her wedding that year.

"Does the press corps know you are home?" Quinn asked, changing the subject. Like him, Cal had a hate-hate affair with the press.

"Everyone knows. They were at the airport and at the hospital."

"Remind me again where you flew in from?" It had been a couple of months since they last spoke and, while they exchanged emails regularly, he couldn't recall where her last project had been. Then again, Cal—as the troubleshooter for her family's foundation—jumped from project to project, country to country, going where she was needed to ensure everything ran smoothly. She could be in Latin America one week and in the Far East the next. Cal collected frequent-flier miles like politicians collected votes.

"Africa. Lesotho, to be precise. I was working on a project to counter soil erosion." Cal nodded toward the center island of the kitchen, to his landline and cell phone. "Your cell rang and then your phone. Mac left a voicemail saying that he and Wren and Kade were on the way over to discuss today's train wreck." She tipped her head and narrowed her amazing, blue-black eyes. "What trouble have you landed yourself in now, Q?"

Quinn heard Mac's and Kade's heavy footsteps on the outside stairs and lifted a shoulder. "You know what they say, Red—the trouble with trouble is that it starts off as fun."

After greeting his best friends—who were also his partners, his colleagues—and Wren, the Mavericks' PR guru, he gestured for them all to take a seat and offered drinks. While he made coffee, Cal was hugged and kissed by his friends and asked how she'd been. It didn't matter how infrequently they saw her, Quinn mused, she automatically slotted back into his life and was immediately accepted because Mac and Kade understood that, just like they did, Cal had his back.

Quinn delivered mugs of coffee and sighed at their doom-and-gloom faces. He could deal with their anxiety—Mac and Kade constantly worried that he'd kill himself chasing his need for adrenaline—but he didn't like their frustration and, yeah, their anger. His teammates and their head of publicity were pissed. Again. Not necessarily at him but at the situation he'd found himself in.

He tended to find himself in a lot of *situations*.

Hell, Quinn thought as he pushed his fingers through

his sweat-dampened hair and gathered it into a knot at the back of his head, *here we go again.*

"Make yourself some coffee, bro. You're going to need it," Mac suggested, leaning back and placing his booted foot on his opposite knee.

"I'll do it," Cal offered.

Though he appreciated her offer, Quinn shook his head. "Thanks, Red, but I've got it."

Quinn ran his hand over his thick beard as he walked around the island into the kitchen to where his coffee machine stood. He picked up his favorite mug, placed it under the spout and pushed the button for a shot of espresso. The machine gurgled, dispensed the caffeine and Quinn hit the button again. He wanted whiskey, but he supposed that a double espresso would have to do.

"So how did the meeting with Warren go?" he asked as he turned around.

Mac, as forthright as ever, gestured to Cal. "Maybe we should do this in private."

Cal immediately stood up and Quinn shook his head. "You know that you can talk in front of Cal. What I know she can know. I trust her."

Mac nodded and rubbed his jaw as Cal sat down again. "Your choice."

"Warren is less than happy with you and he's considering pulling out of the deal."

Quinn gripped the granite island to keep his balance, feeling like a forty-foot wave had passed under the bow of the yacht. *"What?"*

"And why?" Cal demanded, his shock echoed on her face. "What has Quinn done?"

"Is this about the interview Storm gave?" Quinn asked.

"Partly," Kade replied.

Quinn took a sip of his coffee, planted his feet apart and looked out to the water. Earlier in the week he'd woken up to the news that his three-week stand had, a month after he ended it, decided to share the intimate, ugly details of their affair and final breakup. Storm tearfully told the world, on an extremely popular morning breakfast show, that Quinn was emotionally unavailable, that he constantly and consistently cheated on her. For those reasons, she now needed intensive therapy.

None of it was true, but she'd sounded damn convincing.

He'd been played; the world was still being played. He'd made it very clear to her that he wasn't looking for a relationship—and three weeks did not constitute a relationship!—but she'd turned their brief and, to be honest, forgettable affair into a drama. Storm's interview was a massive publicity stunt, the next installment in keeping her admittedly gorgeous face in the news.

"Come and sit down, Quinn," Kade said, gesturing to a chair with his foot. Quinn dropped his long frame into the chair and rested his head on the padded back. His eyes darted from Kade's and Mac's faces to Cal's. Her deep, dark eyes—the exact color of his midnight-blue superbike—reflected worry and concern.

"It's just the latest episode in a series of bad press you've received and Warren is concerned that this is an ongoing trend. He told us, flat out, the Mavericks can't afford any more bad press and that you are the source."

"Does he want me out of the partnership?" Quinn demanded, his heart in his throat.

"He's hinting at it."

Quinn muttered an obscenity. The Mavericks—being Mac and Kade's partner—was what he did and a large part of who he was. Coaching the team was his solace, his hobby and, yeah, his career. He freakin' loved what he did.

But to own and grow the franchise, they needed Bayliss. Bayliss was their link to bigger and better sponsorship deals. He had media connections they could only dream about, connections they needed to grow the Mavericks franchise. But their investor thought Quinn was the weak link.

Craphelldammit.

Quinn looked at Cal and she slid off the barstool to sit on his chair, her arm loosely draped around his shoulders. Damn, he was glad she was back in town, glad she was here. He rarely needed anyone, but right now he needed her.

Her unconditional support, her humor, her solidity.

He looked at Wren, their PR guru. "Is he right? Am I damaging the Mavericks' brand?" he asked, his normally deep voice extra raspy with stress.

Wren flicked her eyes toward the pile of newspapers

beside her. "Well, you're certainly not enhancing it." She linked her hands together on the table and leaned forward, her expression intense. "Basically, all the reports about you lately have followed the same theme and, like a bunch of rabid wolves, the journos are ganging up on you."

Quinn frowned. "Brilliant."

"Unfortunately, they have no reason to treat you kindly. You did nearly run that photographer over a couple of weeks back," Wren said.

Quinn held up his hands. "That was an accident." Sort of.

"And you called the press a collective boil on the ass of humanity during that radio interview."

Well, they were.

Wren continued. "Basically, their theme is that it's time you grew up and that your—let's call them exploits—are getting old and, worse, tiresome. That seeing you with a different woman every month is boring and a cliché. Some journalists are taking this a step further, saying, since Kade and Mac have settled and started families, when are you going to do the same? That what was funny and interesting in your early twenties is now just self-indulgent."

Quinn grimaced. Ouch. Harsh.

Not as harsh as knowing that he'd never be able to have what they had, his own family, but still...

Seriously, Rayne, this *again? For the last five years, you've known about and accepted your infertility! A*

*family is not what you want, remember? Stop thinking
about it and move on!*

Kade picked up a paper and Quinn could see that
someone, probably Wren, had highlighted some text.

Kade read the damaging words out loud. "Our
sources tell us that the deal to buy the Mavericks franchise by Rayne, Kade Webb and Mac McCaskill, and
their investor—the conservative billionaire industri-
alist Warren Bayliss—is about to be finalized. You
would think that Rayne would make an effort to keep
his nose clean. Maybe his partners should tell him that
while he might be a brilliant and successful coach, he
is a shocking example to his players and his personal
life is a joke."

Kade and Mac held his gaze and he respected them
for not dropping their eyes and looking away.

"Is that something you want to tell me?" he
demanded, his voice rough.

Kade exchanged a look with Mac and Mac gestured
for Kade to speak. "The last year has been stressful,
for all of us. So much has happened—Vernon's death,
our partnership with Bayliss, buying the franchise."

"Falling in love, becoming fathers," Wren added.

Kade nodded his agreement. "You generating bad
publicity is complicating the situation. We, specifically
the Mavericks, need you to clean up your act."

Quinn tipped his head back to look at the ceiling.
He wanted to argue, wanted to rage against the unfair
accusations, wanted to shout his denials. Instead, he

dropped his head and looked at Cal, who still sat on the arm of the chair looking thoughtful.

"You've been very quiet, Red. What do you think?"

Cal bit her bottom lip, her eyes troubled. She dropped her head to the side and released a long sigh. "I know how important buying the franchise is and I'd think that you'd want to do whatever you could to make sure that happens." She wrinkled her nose at him. "Maybe you do need to calm down, Q. Stop the serial dating, watch your mouth, stop dueling with death sports—"

The loud jangle of a cell phone interrupted her sentence and Cal hopped up. "Sorry, that's mine. It might be the hospital."

Quinn nodded. Cal bent over to pick up her bag and Quinn blinked as the denim fabric stretched across her perfect, heart-shaped ass. He wiped a hand over his face and swallowed, desperately trying to moisten his mouth. All the blood in his head travelled south to create some action in his pants.

Quinn rubbed the back of his neck. Instead of thinking about Red and her very nice butt, he should be directing his attention to his career. He needed to convince Bayliss he was a necessary and valuable component of the team and not a risk factor. To do that, he had to get the media off his back or, at the very least, get them to focus on something positive about him and his career with the Mavericks. Easy to think; not so easy to do.

As Cal slipped out the glass door onto the smaller

deck, he acknowledged that his sudden attraction to Red was a complication that he definitely could do without.

"Callahan Adam-Carter? Please hold for Mr. Graeme Moore."

Cal frowned, wondered who Graeme Moore was and looked into the lounge behind her, thinking that the three Mavericks men were incredibly sexy. Fit, ripped, cosmopolitan. And since Quinn was the only one who was still single, she wasn't surprised that the press's attention was on him. Breakfast was not breakfast in the city without coffee and the latest gossip about the city's favorite sons.

Over the years his bright blond hair had deepened to the color of rich toffee, but those eyes—those brilliant, ice-green eyes—were exactly the same, edged by long, dark lashes and strong brows. She wasn't crazy about his too-long, dirty-blond beard and his shoulder-length hair, but she could understand why the female population of Vancouver liked his appearance. He looked hard and hot and, as always, very, very masculine. With an edge of danger that immediately had female ovaries twitching. After a lifetime of watching women making fools of themselves over him—tongues dropping, walking into poles, stuttering, stammering, offering to have his babies—she understood that he was a grade-A hottie.

When she was wrapped around him earlier she'd felt her heart rate climb and that special spot between her legs throb. Mmm, interesting. After five years of feeling numb, five years without feeling remotely attracted to anyone, her sexuality was finally creeping back. She'd started to notice men again and she supposed that her reaction to Quinn had everything to do with the fact that it had been a very long time since she'd been up close and personal with a hot man. With any man.

It didn't mean anything. He was Quinn, for God's sake! *Quinn!* This was the same guy who had tried to raise frogs in the family bath, who had teased her mercilessly and defended her from school-yard bullies. To her, he wasn't the youngest but best hockey coach in the NHL, the wild and woolly adrenaline junkie who provided grist for the tabloids, or the ripped bad boy who dated supermodels and publicity-seeking actresses.

He was just Quinn, her closest friend for the best part of twenty years.

Well, eighteen years, to be precise. They hadn't spoken to each other for six months before her wedding or at any time during her marriage. It was only after Toby's death that they'd reconnected.

"Mrs. Carter, I'm glad I've finally reached you."

Mrs. Carter? Cal's stomach contracted and her coffee made its way back up her throat. She swallowed and swallowed again.

"I've sent numerous messages to your email address at Carter International, but you have yet to respond," Moore continued. "I heard you were back in the country so I finally tracked down your cell number."

Cal shrugged. Her life had stopped the day Toby died and she seldom—okay, never—paid attention to messages sent to that address.

"I'm sorry. Who are you?"

"Toby Carter's lawyer and I'm calling about his estate."

"I don't understand why, since Toby's estate was settled years ago," Cal said, frowning.

Moore remained silent for a long time and he eventually spoke again. "I read his will after the funeral, Mrs. Carter. Do you remember that day?"

No, not really. Her memory of Toby's death and burial was shrouded in a mist she couldn't—didn't want to—penetrate.

"I handed you a folder, asked you to read the will again when you felt stronger," Moore continued when she failed to answer him. "You didn't do that, did you?"

Cal pushed away the nauseating emotions that swirled to the surface whenever she thought or talked about Toby and forced herself to think. And no, she hadn't read the will again. She didn't even remember the folder. It was probably where she left it, in the study at Toby's still-unoccupied house.

"Why are you calling me, Mr. Moore?"

"This is a reminder that Mr. Carter's estate has been in abeyance for the last five years. Mr. Carter wanted you to inherit, but he didn't want to share his wealth with your future spouse. His will states that if you have not remarried five years after his death, you inherit his estate."

"What?"

"His estate includes his numerous bank accounts, his properties—both here and overseas—and his shares in Carter International. Also included are his art, furniture and gemstone collections. The estate is valued in the region of $200 million."

"I don't want it. I don't want anything! Give it to his sons."

"The will cannot be changed and his assets cannot be transferred. If you remarry before the anniversary of his death, then you will no longer be a beneficiary of Mr. Carter's will and only then will his estate be split evenly between his two sons."

Toby, you scumbag. "So I have to marry within four months to make sure that his sons inherit what they are—morally and ethically—entitled to?" Cal demanded, feeling her heart thud against her rib cage.

"Exactly."

"Do you know how nuts this is?"

After begging her to read his emails, Moore ended the call. Cal closed her eyes and pulled in deep breaths, flooding her lungs with air in order to push back the panic. Everything Toby owned was tainted, covered with the same deep, dark, controlling and possessive energy that he'd concealed beneath the charming, urbane, kind personality he showed the world.

Cal scrunched her eyelids closed, trying not to remember the vicious taunting, her confusion, the desperation. He was five years dead and he could still make her panic, make her doubt herself, turn her hard-fought independence into insecurity. She couldn't be his heir. She didn't want to own anything of his. She never wanted to be linked to him again.

To remain mentally and emotionally free of her husband, she couldn't be tied to anything he owned. She'd marry the first man she could to rid herself of his contaminated legacy.

Cal turned as she heard the door to the lounge slide open and saw Quinn standing there. She pulled a smile onto her face and hoped that Quinn was too involved in his own drama to notice that she'd taken a starring role in one of her own.

Quinn frowned at her, obviously seeing something on her face or in her eyes to make him pause. "Everything okay?" he asked as he gestured her inside.

Cal nodded as she walked back into the lounge.

"Apart from the fact that I need a husband, I'm good." Cal saw the shocked expressions that followed and waved her comment away. "Bad joke. Ignore me. So, have you found a solution to your problem? Any ideas on how to get Quinn some good press?"

Wren leaned forward and crossed her legs, linking her hands over her knees, her expression thoughtful. "I wish you weren't joking, Cal. Quinn marrying you would be excellent PR for him."

Mac and Kade laughed, Quinn spluttered, but Cal just lifted her eyebrows in a tell-me-more expression.

"You're PR gold, Callahan. You are the only child of a fairy-tale romance between your superrich father and Rachel Thomas, the principal soloist with the Royal Canadian Ballet Company, who is considered one of the world's best ballerinas. You married Toby Carter, the most elusive and eligible of Vancouver's bachelors until these three knuckleheads came along. The public loves you to distraction, despite the fact that you are seldom in the city."

Could she? Did she dare? It would be a quick, convenient solution.

Cal gathered her courage, pulled on her brightest smile and turned to Quinn. "So, what do you think? Want to get married?"

Two

Cal called a final good-bye to Quinn's friends and closed the sliding door behind them. She walked through the main salon, passed the large dining table and hesitated at the steps that would take her belowdecks to the sleeping cabins below. Quinn had hurried down those stairs after she'd dropped her bombshell but not before telling her that her suggestion that they marry was deeply unamusing and wildly inappropriate.

She hadn't been joking and the urge to run downstairs and explain was strong. But Cal knew Quinn, knew that he needed some time alone to work through his temper, to gather his thoughts. She did too. To give them both a little time, she walked back into the kitchen and snagged a microbrew from his stash in the fridge.

Twisting the top off, she took a swallow straight from the bottle. She'd been back in Vancouver for less than a day and she already felt like the city had a feather pillow over her face.

Being back in Vancouver always did that to her; the city she'd loved as a child, a teenager and a young woman now felt like it was trying to smother her.

Cal pulled a face. As pretty as Quinn's new yacht was, she didn't want to be here. A square inch of her heart—the inch that was pure bitch—resented having to come back here, resented leaving the anonymity of the life she'd created after Toby. But her father needed her here and since he was the only family she had left, she'd caught the first flight home.

Cal ran the cold bottle over her cheek and closed her eyes. When she was away from Vancouver, she was Cal Adam and she had little connection to Callahan Adam-Carter, Toby's young, socially connected, perfectly pedigreed bride. Despite the fact that she stood to inherit her father's wealth, she was as far removed from the wife she'd been as politicians were from the truth. The residents of her hometown would be shocked to realize that she was now as normal as any single, almost-thirty-year-old widowed woman who'd grown up in the public eye could be.

She'd worked hard to chase her freedom, to live independently, to find her individuality. It hadn't always been easy. She was the only child of one of the country's richest men, the widow of another rich, wildly popular man and the daughter of a beloved icon of the dance world. Her best friend was also the city's favorite bad boy.

To whom, on a spur-of-the-moment suggestion, she'd just proposed marriage. Crazy!

Yet…yet in a small, pure part of her brain, it made complete sense on a number of levels and in the last few years she'd learned to listen to that insistent voice.

First, and most important, marrying her would be a good move for Quinn. She was reasonably pretty, socially connected and the reporters and photographers loved her. She was also so rarely in the city that whatever she did, or said, was guaranteed to garner coverage. In a nutshell, she sold newspapers, online or print. Being linked with her, being *married* to her, would send a very strong message that Quinn was turning his life around.

Because nobody—not even Quinn Rayne, legendary bad boy—would play games with Callahan Adam-Carter. And, as a bonus, her father and Warren Bayliss did a lot of business together, so Bayliss wouldn't dare try excluding Cauley's son-in-law from any deal involving the other two Mavericks.

Yeah, marrying her would be a very good move on Quinn's part.

As for her…

If she wanted no part of Toby's inheritance, then she needed to marry. That was nonnegotiable. And in order to protect herself, to protect her freedom and independence, she needed to marry a man who was safe, someone she could be honest with. She knew Quinn and trusted him. He lived life on his own terms and, since he hated restrictions, he was a live-and-let-live type of guy. Just the type of man—*the only type of man*—she could ever consider marrying.

Quinn wouldn't rock her emotional boat. She'd known him all her life, and never thought of him in any way but as her friend. The little spark she'd felt earlier was an aberration and not worth considering, so marrying him would be an easy way out of her sticky situation. No mess, no fuss.

And if she took over the management of the foundation for a while and found herself back in the social swirl, being Quinn's wife would assuage some highbrow curiosity about her change from an insecure, meek, jump-at-shadows girl to the stronger, assertive, more confident woman she now was. Nobody would expect Quinn—the Mavericks' Bad Boy—to have a mousy wife.

This marriage—presuming she could get Quinn to agree—would be in name only. Nothing between them would change. It would be a marriage of convenience, a way to help to free herself from Toby's tainted legacy.

It would be a ruse, a temporary solution to both their problems. It would be an illusion, a show, a production—

but the heart of their friendship, of who they were, would stay the same.

It had to. Anything else would be unacceptable.

Provided, of course, that she could get Quinn to agree.

Was she out of her mind? Had she left the working part of her brain in… God, where had she been? Some tiny, landlocked African country he couldn't remember the name of. No matter—what the hell was Cal thinking?

Quinn had been so discombobulated by her prosaic, seemingly serious proposal that he'd shouted at her to stop joking around and told his mates that he was going to take a shower, hoping that some time alone under the powerful sprays of his double-head shower would calm him down.

It was the most relaxing shower system in the world, his architect had promised him. Well, relaxing, his ass.

He simply wasn't marriage and family material. God, he was barely part of the family he grew up within, and now Cal was suggesting that they make one together?

Cal had definitely taken her seat on the crazy train.

But if she was, if the notion was so alien to him, why did his stomach twitch with excitement at the thought? Why did he sometimes—when he felt tired or stressed—wish he had someone to come home to, a family to distract him from the stresses of being the youngest, least experienced head coach in the league?

And, worst of all, why, when he saw Kade and Mac with their women, did he feel, well, squirrelly, like something, maybe, possibly, was missing from his life?

Nah, it was gas or indigestion or an approaching heart attack—he couldn't possibly be jealous of the happiness he saw in their eyes... Besides, Cal had only suggested marriage, not the added extras.

It was a normal reaction to not wanting to be alone, he decided, reaching for the shampoo and savagely dumping far too much in his open palm, cursing when most of it fell to the floor. He viciously rubbed what was left over his long hair and his beard and swore when some suds burned his eyes. Turning the jets as far as they could go, he ducked and allowed the water to pummel his head, his face, his shoulders. Marriage, family, kids—all impossible. Seven years ago, during a routine team checkup, he'd been told by the team doctor and a specialist that his blood tests indicated there was a 95 percent chance he was infertile. Further tests were suggested, but Quinn, not particularly fazed, hadn't bothered. He'd quickly moved on from the news and that was what he needed to do again. *Like, right now. Is it time for you to grow up, Rayne?*

His friends' lives were changing and because of that, his should too. Quinn swore, his curses bouncing off the bathroom walls. But, unfair or not, the fact was that his liaison with Storm, his daredevil stunts, his laissez-faire attitude to everything but his coaching and training of the team, had tarnished the image of the Mavericks and

Bayliss didn't want him to be part of the deal. If Kade and Mac decided to side with him and ditch Bayliss as an investor, there was a very real chance that the Widow Hasselback would sell the franchise to Chenko. And that would be on Quinn's head.

His teammates, his friends, his brothers didn't deserve that.

He didn't have a choice. He'd sacrifice his free-wheelin' lifestyle, clean up his mouth, tone down the crazy stunts, exhibit some patience and stop giving the press enough rope to hang him. Mac and Kade, his players, the fans— everyone needed him to pull a rabbit out of his hat and that's what he would do. But how long would it take for the press to get off his ass? Three months? Six? He could behave himself for as long as he needed to, but it would mean no stunts, no women...

No women. After Storm's crazy-as-hell behavior, he was happy to date himself for a while. And the new season was about to start. With draft picks and fitness assessments and training, he wouldn't have that much spare time. Yeah, he could take a break from the sweeter-smelling species for a while, easily.

What he wouldn't do is get married. That was crazy talk. Besides, Cal had been joking. She had a weird, offbeat sense of humor.

Quinn shut off the jets, grabbed a towel and wound it around his hips. He walked out of his bathroom and braked the moment he saw Cal sitting on the edge of his king-sized bed, a beer bottle in her hand.

"Just make yourself at home, sunshine," he drawled, sarcasm oozing from every clean pore.

"We should get married," she told him, a light of determination in her eyes.

He recognized that look. Cal had her serious-as-hell face on. "God, Cal! Have you lost your mind?"

Possibly.

Cal watched as Quinn disappeared into his walk-in closet and slammed the door behind him. She eyed the closed door and waited for him to reemerge, knowing that she needed to make eye contact with Quinn to make him realize how desperately serious she was.

Dear Lord, the man had a six-pack that could make a woman weep. Callahan Adam, get a grip! You've seen Quinn in just a towel before. Hell, you've seen him naked before! This should not—he should not—be able to distract you!

Right. Focus.

Them getting married was a temporary, brilliant solution to both their problems, but she'd have to coax, persuade and maybe bully him into tying the knot with her. If she and Quinn married, she would be killing a flock of pesky pigeons with one supercharged, magic stone. She just needed Quinn to see the big picture…

The door to the closet opened and Quinn walked out, now dressed in a pair of straight-legged track pants and a long-sleeved T-shirt, the arms pushed up to reveal the muscles in his forearms. He'd brushed his hair off his face, but his scowl remained.

Cal sat cross-legged in the middle of the bed and patted the comforter next to her. "Let's chat."

"Let's not if you're going to mention the word *marriage*." Quinn scowled and sat on the edge of the bucket chair in the corner, his elbows on his knees and his expression as dark as the night falling outside. Oh, she recognized the stubbornness in his eyes. He wasn't in any mood to discuss her on-the-fly proposal. If she pushed him now, he'd dig in his heels and she'd end up inheriting Toby's tainted $200 million.

Being a little stubborn herself, she knew that the best way to handle Quinn was to back off and approach the problem from another angle.

Cal rubbed her eyes with her fist. "It's been a really crazy afternoon. And a less-than-wonderful day. I spoke to my dad's doctor about fifteen minutes ago."

Quinn's demeanor immediately changed from irritation to concern. He leaned forward, his concentration immediately, absolutely, focused on her. It was one of his most endearing traits. If you were his friend and he cared about you and you said that you were in trouble that was all that was important. "And? Is he okay?"

"He looked awful, so very old," Cal said, placing her beer bottle on his bedside table. Her father would be okay, she reminded herself as panic climbed up her throat. The triple heart bypass had been successful and he just needed time to recover.

"The doctor says he needs to take three months off. He needs to be stress-free for that time. He's recommended my father book into a private, very exclusive recovery center in Switzerland."

"But?"

"According to the doc, Dad is worried about the foundation. Apparently, there are loads of fund-raisers soon—the annual masked ball, the half-marathon, the art auction. The doctor said that if I want my father to make a full recovery, I'll have to find someone to take over his responsibilities."

"There's only one person he'd allow to step into his shoes," Quinn stated, stretching out his legs and leaning back in his chair.

"Me."

"You're an Adam, Red, and your father has always held the view that the foundation needs an Adam face. I remember him giving you a thirty-minute monologue over dinner about how the contributors and the grant recipients valued that personal connection. How old were we? Fifteen?"

Cal smiled. "Fourteen."

"So are you going to run the foundation for him?"

"How can I not?" Cal replied. "It's three months. I spent three months building houses in Costa Rica, in Haiti after their earthquake, in that refugee camp in Sudan. I say yes to helping strangers all the time. I want to say yes to helping my father, but I don't want to stay in Vancouver. I want be anywhere but here. But if I do stay here, then I can help you, Q. Marrying me will help you rehab your reputation."

If this wasn't so damn serious, then she'd be tempted to laugh at his horrified expression.

"I'm not interested in using my association with you, sullying my friendship with you, to improve my PR," Quinn told her in his take-no-prisoners voice.

And there was that streak of honor so few people saw but was a fundamental part of Quinn. He did his own thing, but he made sure his actions didn't impact anyone else. His integrity—his honor—was why she couldn't believe a word his psycho ex spouted about their relationship. Quinn didn't play games, didn't obfuscate, didn't lie. And he never, ever, made promises he couldn't keep.

"I can rehabilitate my own reputation without help from you or anyone else."

Cal didn't disagree with him; Quinn could do anything he set his mind to. "Of course you can, but it would be a lot quicker if you let me help you. The reality is that, according to the world, I am the good girl and you're the bad boy. I don't drink, party or get caught with my panties down." God, she sounded so boring, so blah. "I am seen to be living a productive and meaningful life. I am the poster girl for how filthy-rich heiresses should behave."

"Bully for you," Quinn muttered, looking unimpressed.

"I know—I sound awful, don't I?" Cal wrinkled her

nose. "But my rep, or the lack of it, can work for you, if you let it. Being seen with me, spending time with me will go a long way to restoring your reputation and, right now, it needs some polishing. The Mavericks are in sensitive discussions around the future of the team and, from what I can gather, your position within the organization is unstable. Your fans are jittery. You're about to start a new season and, as the coach, you need them behind you and you need them to trust you. They probably don't at the moment."

A muscle ticked in his jaw. She was hurting him, and she was sorry for that. His job—his career—was everything to him and her words were like digging a knife into a bullet wound.

"If we're married, the world will look at you and think, 'Hey, he's with Callahan, and we all know that she has her feet on the ground. Maybe we've been a bit tough on him.' Or maybe they'll think that your exploits couldn't have been that bad if I'm prepared to be with you. Whatever they interpret from the two of us being together, it should be positive."

"I cannot believe that we are still discussing this, but—" Quinn frowned "—why marriage? Why would we have to go that far? Why couldn't we just be in a relationship?"

Cal took a minute to come up with a response that made sense. "Because if we just pretend to have a relationship, then it could be interpreted as me being another notch on your belt, another of your bang-her-

'til-you're-bored women. No, you have to be taken seriously and what's more serious than marriage?"

Quinn frowned at her. "Death? Or isn't that the same thing?"

"I'm not suggesting a life sentence, Quinn."

"And would this be a fake marriage or a let's-get-the-legal-system-involved marriage?"

Cal considered his question. "It would be easier if it was fake, but some intrepid journalist would check and if they find out we're trying to snow them, they'll go ballistic. If we do this, then we have to do it properly."

"I'm over the moon with excitement."

Cal ignored his sarcasm. "I'm thinking that we stay married for about a year, maybe eighteen months. We act, when we're out in public, like this is the real deal. Behind closed doors we'll be who we always are, best friends. After the furor has died down, after the Mavericks purchase is complete, we'll start to go our own ways and, after a while, we'll separate. Then we'll have a quick and quiet divorce, saying that we are better off as friends and that we still love each other, all of which will be true."

Quinn narrowed his eyes at her. "That's a hell of a plan, Red. And why do you want to do this?"

And that's where this got tricky, Cal thought. Without a detailed explanation, he wouldn't understand her wish to walk away from so much money. She'd have to explain that accepting Toby's money would stain her soul and Quinn would demand to know why.

She couldn't tell him that the debonair, sophisticated, charming and besotted-by-his-new-bride Toby turned into a psycho behind closed doors.

She simply couldn't tell anyone. Some topics, she was convinced, never needed to see the light of day.

"Being part of a couple provides me with a barrier to hide behind when the demands of my father's high-society world become too much. I need to be able to re-fuse invitations to cocktail parties and events, to not go to dinner with eligible men, to do the minimal amount of socializing that is required of me. In order to get away with that without offending anyone, I need a good ex-cuse." Her mouth widened into a smile. "My brand-new husband would be an excellent excuse."

Quinn closed his eyes. "You're asking me to marry you so you can duck your social obligations? Do you know how lame that sounds?"

It did sound lame, even to her. "Sure, but it will stop me from going nuts."

"The press will be all over us like a rash." Quinn said.

"Yeah, but, after a couple of weeks, they will move on to something else and will, hopefully, leave us alone."

Quinn didn't look convinced and stared at the carpet beneath his feet. "What happens if we do get married and you meet someone who you want to spend the rest of your life with?"

Jeez, she was never getting married—in the real

sense—ever again. She'd never hand a man that much control over her, allow him to have that much input into how she lived her life. She'd been burned once, scorched, *incinerated*—there was no way she'd play with fire again. Marrying Quinn was just a smoke screen and nothing would change, not really. They had everything to gain and little to lose.

"Don't worry about that. Look, all I'm asking is for you to provide me with a shield between my father's world and the pound of flesh they want from me," Cal stated. "It's taking the lemons life gives you—"

"If you say anything about making lemonade, I might strangle you," Quinn warned her in his super-growly, super-sexy voice.

Cal grinned. "Hell, no! When life gives me lemons, I slice those suckers up, haul out the salt and tequila and do shots." She stretched out her legs. "So, are we going to get married or what, Rayne?"

He stood up and stretched, and the hem of his shirt pulled up to reveal furrows of hard stomach muscle and a hint of those long, vertical muscles over his hips that made woman say—and do—stupid things. Like taking a nip right there, heading lower to take his...

Cal slammed her eyes shut and hauled in some much-needed air. Had she really fantasized about kissing Quinn...*there*? She waited for the wave of shame, but nothing happened. Well, she was still wondering how good those muscles and his masculine skin would feel under her hands, on her tongue.

She had to get out of his bedroom. *Now.* Before she did something stupid like slapping her mouth on his. Her libido wasn't gently creeping back; it was galloping in on a white stallion, naked and howling.

Maybe getting hitched wasn't the brightest idea she'd ever had. She should backtrack, tell Quinn that this was a crazy-bad idea, that she'd changed her mind.

"Okay, let's do it," Quinn said. "Let's get hitched."

Oh, damn. Too late.

Three

Three weeks later...

Cal, yawning, stumbled up the stairs, her eyes half closed and her brain still in sleep mode. A cool wind from an open door whirled around her and she rubbed her hands over her arms, thinking that she should've pulled a robe over her skimpy camisole and boy shorts. Coffee time, she decided.

Cal looked to her right, her attention caught by the silver-pink sheen as the sun danced on the sea. Maybe she wouldn't go back to bed. Maybe she'd go up onto the deck and watch the sun wake up and a new day bloom.

"Morning."

Cal screeched, whirled around and slapped her hand

on her chest. Quinn stood in the galley kitchen, a pair of low-slung boxers hanging off his slim hips, long hair pulled into a tail at the back of his neck. Oh, God, he was practically naked and her eyes skimmed over the acre of male muscles. His shoulders seemed broader this morning, his arms bigger, that six-pack more defined. She—slowly, it had to be said—lifted her eyes to his face. Her heart bounced off her rib cage when she realized his eyes were on her bare legs and were moving, ever so slowly, north. She felt her internal temperature rocket up and her nipples pucker when his eyes lingered on her chest. When their eyes met, she thought she saw desire—hot and hard—flicker in his eyes and across his face. But it came and went so quickly that she doubted herself; after all, it wasn't like she'd had a lot of experience with men and attraction lately. Lately, as in the past five years.

Her libido had picked a fine time to get with the program, she decided, deeply disgusted. It was a special type of hell being attracted to your fake husband.

"Do you want coffee?" Quinn said as he turned his back to her. Cal heard an extra rasp in his voice that raised goosebumps on her skin. His back view was almost as good as the front view—an amazing butt, defined and muscular shoulders, a straight spine. There was also a solid inch of white skin between his tanned back and the band of his plain black boxers.

Cal placed her hand on her forehead as she tried to convince herself that she wasn't attracted to him,

that she was being ridiculous. She forced herself to remember that she'd seen him eat week-old pizza, that he
was revolting when he was hungover and he sounded
like he was killing a cat when he sang. She told herself that she'd never felt even marginally attracted to
him so whatever she was feeling was flu or pneumo-
nia or typhoid.

Her libido just laughed at her.

"Red, coffee?"

Quinn's question jolted her back and she managed
to push a *yes* through her lips. Cal crossed her arms
over her chest and felt her hard nipples pressing into
her fisted hands. Dammit, she needed to cover up. She
couldn't walk around half-dressed. Cal looked toward
the salon and saw a light throw lying across the back
of one couch. She quickly walked across the room to
wrap it around her shoulders and instantly felt calmer,
more in control.

Less likely to strip and jump him in the kitchen…

"Here you go."

Cal turned and smiled her thanks as Quinn placed
a coffee mug on the island counter. Keeping the ends
of the throw gathered at her chest, she walked toward
him and pushed her other hand through the opening
to pick up her cup. She took a grateful sip and sighed.
Great coffee.

"I'm surprised to see you up and about so early,"
Quinn said, turning away to fix his own cup.

"Couldn't sleep," Cal replied.

Quinn lifted his mug to his mouth and gestured to the short flight of stairs that led to the upper deck. "Let's go up. It's a nice place to start the day."

On the deck Cal sat down on the closest blocky settee, placed her coffee cup on the wooden deck and wrapped her arms around her bent legs. She turned and watched as Quinn walked up the stairs, cup and an apple in his hands. He'd pulled on a black hooded sweatshirt and disappointment warred with relief.

Quinn sat down next to her, put his mug next to hers and took a big bite from his apple. They didn't speak for a while, happy to watch the sun strengthen, bouncing off the tip of the mountains on one side and the skyscrapers on the other.

She'd forgotten how truly beautiful Vancouver could be. And sitting here, feeling the heat radiating off Quinn's big body, she enjoyed the quiet. When they decided to marry, they'd stepped into a whirlwind of their own creation. Between dealing with the press, her responsibilities to the foundation and the beginning of the new hockey season for him, they had barely touched base since their quick Vegas wedding. And, despite her moving into the guest cabin downstairs, she hardly saw him.

That could be because he was already gone when she woke up and the nights when she knew he was in, she made a concerted effort to be somewhere else.

Cal had the sneaking suspicion that he was also avoiding her and wondered why. She knew what her reasons were—she'd prefer that he didn't realize that she lusted after him, that she spent many nights in her cabin imagining what making love with him would be like. She didn't want to complicate this situation, make it any more uncomfortable than it already was and, man, it was complicated enough already.

Cal lifted her cup to her mouth, the diamond in her engagement ring flashing despite the still-low light. Then again, at ten carats, the ring could be seen from space.

"How are things?" Cal asked Quinn, noting his tired eyes. "I haven't seen you since we attended that art exhibition two nights ago."

"Where we spoke to the press more than we spoke to each other," Quinn said, his expression enigmatic.

Cal shook her head, disgusted. "I expected some interest around my return, but this is ridiculous. And, if I'm out alone, they're always asking where you are."

"How do you answer?"

"I say that you're at home, naked, waiting for me to ravish you," Cal joked, but, instead of laughing something indefinable flashed in his eyes. Cal felt her mouth dry up. She waved her coffee cup and brushed the flash of whatever that was away. "I tell them that we both have very busy lives, that you're working."

"Well, that's the truth. I do little else but work. It's the start of the season and I have a young team who need extra practice."

"I saw that you have some new players on board. They any good?"

"If they weren't, they wouldn't be there," Quinn replied. "I might not take much seriously, but I don't mess around with the team."

Cal lifted her eyebrows at his touchy tone. Quinn was normally easygoing, tolerant and charming. Hearing him snap was always a surprise. She understood his frustration. Quinn didn't function well when he was bound by rules, when he felt like he had clipped wings. Wren, the Mavericks' PR whiz, had carefully choreographed every aspect of their fake marriage, from the leaked photographs of their quickie wedding to their appearances on the social scene. Someone having that much control of his personal life would rub Quinn raw.

Their marriage grounded him, but Quinn desperately needed to fly. Unfortunately, he'd been flying too close to the sun for far too long. "It's not forever, Quinn. You'll be rid of me before you know it."

Beneath his beard, Quinn's white teeth flashed. "Honey, I saw more of you via Skype when you were halfway across the world than I do now and you're living on my damn yacht. Though, in some ways, that's not a bad thing."

Okay, she was not touching that cryptic statement with a barge pole. "Maybe you and I need to reconnect, *as friends*. We need to remember that before we were caught up in this craziness, we enjoyed each other's company. Let's make some time try to be who we always were."

And if they managed to reconnect as friends, maybe this ridiculous need to touch him, to taste him would disappear. God, she could only hope. "When are you free?"

Quinn frowned, thinking. "Tonight I have plans. Tomorrow night I'm having drinks with some potential sponsors. Thursday is poker night."

Once-a-month poker night with Kade and Mac was sacrosanct. Even Brodie, Kade's fiancée, was under strict instructions to not go into labor until Friday morning.

Boys.

"Friday?" Quinn asked, lifting his startling eyes back to her face. God, she loved his eyes.

Friday? *Really?* "That would work except for one little thing."

"What?"

"Friday is the Adam Foundation Masked Ball. It's only the most important social event on the city's calendar."

Quinn pulled a face. "And I suppose I *have* to be there?"

"Q, I'm the official host and you're my husband!"

"I'll be masked. How will they even know that I'm there? I could be anyone," Quinn protested.

"Yeah, there will be so many six-foot-three ripped men there with long blond hair and beards. C'mon,

Quinn, you *knew* about this. I sent you an email about it last week."

"Ugh."

"Have you got a mask yet?"

Quinn sent her a get-real look and Cal sighed. Of course he hadn't; he'd heard the words *mask* and *ball* and tuned out. "Leave it to me."

"Plain black, as small as possible," Quinn growled. "Do not make me look like an idiot."

"The point of the masked ball is to be masked, as much as possible. Not knowing who is behind the mask is part of the fun," Cal protested. Knowing that choosing a mask would be pure torture for him, she'd already purchased a plain black affair that covered three quarters of his face. It was, she and Wren agreed, as fussy as Quinn would tolerate. "Relax. Plain black tuxedo, black tie and the mask. That's it."

Quinn made a sound in the back of his throat that sounded like a rhino going into labor. She patted his shoulder and smiled. "Quinn, it's a masked ball, not a root canal."

Quinn reached out and tugged her ponytail. "So what are you wearing?"

Cal looked down into her empty coffee cup, wondering if she should tell him about the dress she'd found in a tiny boutique in Gastown. Maybe not, because she still wasn't sure whether she'd have the guts to wear it. It was a kick-ass dress and not something her husband's friends and acquaintances would expect her to wear.

It would make heads turn and tongues wag and probably not in a good way. But no one would mistake her message: Callahan Adam-Carter had died with her husband, but Cal Adam—or Cal Adam-Rayne to be precise—was back in town. "I'm not sure yet," she hedged.

"Whatever you wear, I know you'll look fantastic. You always do."

Cal tipped her head and flushed at his words. It wasn't an empty compliment or a line. Quinn said the words easily and with conviction. He genuinely believed them. God, it was such a silly thing, but such easy acceptance meant the world to her.

"So what time do you want to leave for the ball?" Quinn asked.

Cal lifted his wrist to look at the face of his high-tech watch. She was going to be late for her early meeting if she didn't get cracking. "I'll find you there, somewhere. I have to be there early to check on everything, so you can get there later. Or come with Mac and Kade. Anyway, I have to go," Cal told him, leaning sideways to place a kiss on his cheek.

She inhaled his scent and instantly felt calmer, his arm under her fingers tight with muscle. God, her best friend—her fake husband—was all heat and harnessed power. Their eyes clashed and an emotion she didn't recognize flashed between them. Quinn's eyes dropped to her mouth and she touched her top lip with the tip of her tongue.

Quinn lifted his hand, bent his head and for one

brief, red-hot second Cal thought that he would, finally, give her the kiss she was aching for. She waited, but Quinn just sucked in a harsh-sounding breath, pulled back and abruptly stood up.

Cal bent over to pick up both their cups, stood and walked to the stairs. "I'll see you at the ball, okay?" she said, her voice wobbly as she tossed the words over her shoulder.

"Sure," Quinn answered, sounding absolutely normal. So why did she sense—wish—that he was looking at her butt as she walked away?

It was later in the morning and Mac warbled a horrible version of the "Wedding March" tune as Quinn walked into the conference room at the Mavericks' headquarters. He handed Mac a sour look and frowned at Kade.

"What?" Kade asked, looking confused. "What did I do?"

"You instituted the ban on getting physical anywhere other than the ice or the gym," Quinn complained, dropping his helmet onto the seat of an empty chair. "If it wasn't for you, then I could shut him up."

"You really should see someone about those delusions, dude." Mac smiled.

Standing opposite Mac, Quinn placed his hands flat on the table, leaned across it and got up in his face. "And I swear, if I hear that stupid song one more time, I will rip you a new one, Kade's ban be damned."

Mac just laughed at him. "You can try, bro, you can try. So how is married life?"

Quinn pulled back, blew out his breath and tried to hold onto his temper. He had this conversation at least once a day and he was thoroughly sick of it. *What type of question was that anyway?* he silently fumed. What he and Cal got up to behind closed doors—which was nothing that would make a nun blush—was nobody's business but their own. Yet their marriage fascinated everybody, from his friends to the general public.

And why was Mac asking? He knew that their marriage was as fake as the tooth fairy. Quinn sent Mac an assessing look and decided to play him at his own game. "Actually, Cal and I had hot sex on the deck in the moonlight."

"Seriously?" Mac's face lit up with amusement.

"No, butthead, we didn't." Quinn looked at his helmet and wondered if he could use it to bash some sense into Mac's thick skull. He dropped into a chair, placed his elbows on the table and shoveled his hands into his hair. *"Dude,"* he moaned, feeling a headache brewing, "I don't know how else to explain this to you... Cal and I have been friends since we were in kindergarten. We are not going to sleep together. This is a sham marriage, one we entered to achieve a very specific objective. Remember?"

"What's the point of being hitched if you don't, at the very least, get some fun out of it? And by fun I mean sex."

Quinn didn't respond, knowing that Mac was just looking for a reaction. And they had the temerity to tell him that *he* needed to grow up?

"The point of their marriage was to rehab his reputation and that is going exceptionally well." Wren's cool voice brought a measure of intelligence to their conversation and Quinn could've kissed her.

"Really?" he asked.

Wren sent him a sympathetic smile. "Really. The press has definitely warmed up to you and Bayliss doesn't think you are the spawn of Satan anymore."

"Yay," Quinn said, hiding his relief under sarcasm.

Once he agreed to sell his soul to the devil—aka Wren and her publicity machine—he'd placed his life into Wren's very capable hands. She'd organized every detail of their wedding and made it look like a hasty, romantic, impulsive affair. The woman was damn good. No one suspected that it was a highly orchestrated con.

"And, despite some initial reservations about you and Cal, and how good you will be for her, the public sees your marriage as a positive thing." Wren's eyes left his face and dropped to the sheaf of papers on the table in front of her and Quinn knew there was more she wanted to say and she was debating whether she should or not.

Quinn rubbed the space between his eyebrows. "What, Wren?"

Wren lifted one shoulder in a shrug. "A good portion of the public is just waiting for you to mess it up."

Quinn threw his hands up in the air. "What can I

mess up? You've banned me from doing anything that might raise an eyebrow. I'm married so I can't date." Quinn shook his head and looked at the broad band on his left hand. "That sounds insane."

"You do have a knack of complicating the hell out of your life, Rayne," Kade agreed.

That was the thing. He really didn't. His life, as he saw it, was uncomplicated: he went to work, coached the hell out of the Mavericks and got results that nobody expected from a young coach with little experience. So why couldn't they keep their hands, and their opinions, off his personal life? He kept it simple there too: he did what he wanted, when he wanted.

Well, except for this episode of his life. He really hadn't wanted to get married...

You're temporarily *hitched,* temporarily *grounded and for a damn good reason.* When he remembered what was at risk, he would stay married and well-behaved forever if that was what was required of him.

He would not be the reason the deal with Widow Hasselback failed. He would not give Bayliss a reason to pull out of the deal. He'd protect his team, his players, the brand. He'd protect the Mavericks with everything he had.

Because this place, this team, these men were his home. Yeah, technically, he had a family, but he hadn't spoken to any of them for years. A lack of understanding, communication and, okay, kindness had forced him to distance himself from them and it was a decision he did not regret. Kade and Mac, as annoying as they could be, were now his brothers and he would, at some point—*soon!*—go back to thinking of Cal as the sister he'd never had.

Cal, Mac and Kade were all the family he needed—the only family he'd ever have. He wasn't going to risk Cal not being part of his clan, part of his life, by acting on what was a frequent and annoying fantasy of stripping her naked and making her scream.

Quinn scowled up at the ceiling. His simmering attraction to Cal was unexplainable and ludicrous and it would pass—he just had to keep avoiding her as much as possible until it did—and their friendship would survive. This craziness would pass. Everything always did.

Quinn rolled his shoulders and felt like the walls were closing in on him. He imagined himself on his bike, leaning into a corner, the wind blowing his restlessness away.

"Oh, crap, he has that faraway look in his eyes. The one he gets when he's feeling caged in."

Mac's words penetrated Quinn's fog and he snapped his head up to glare at his friend. "What are you talking about?"

"It's one of your tells," Mac informed him. "You get glassy-eyed and we know that you're considering doing something crazy."

"I'm not going to do anything." Quinn pushed the

words out. He wanted to. He wanted to burn some of this excess energy off. But he wouldn't. Not today anyway.

"Don't mess up, Rayne. Please don't jeopardize our hard work." Kade's words felt like bullets from a machine gun.

Ben is studying, Quinn. Don't disturb Jack.

Try to be more considerate, Quinn.

Why can't you toe the line, Quinn? Be more like your brothers, Quinn? Why do you have to be so much trouble, Quinn?

It was stupid and crazy and childish, but statements like *don't rock the boat, Quinn* and *be good, Quinn* just made him want to do the opposite. He loathed being told what to do. Quinn bit the inside of his lip and jammed his hands into the pockets of his leather jacket so his friends couldn't see his clenched fists.

He wasn't in control of his own life and he despised it and, yes, Kade was right—he did want to run.

It's not for long, Quinn told himself for the umpteenth time. In six months he could start, to a certain extent, living life on his own terms again.

"Sit your ass down, Rayne, and let's get to work," Kade told him and it took Quinn a moment, or twenty, to obey.

The Adam Foundation's masquerade ball was touted as "A sexy, masked Venetian affair" and Quinn thought most of the guests were taking the suggestion that they come disguised a little too far.

Elaborate wigs and masks effectively hid identities, allowing their wearers the anonymous freedom to indulge in some hard-core flirting and, if they wanted to, to go beyond flirting in the dark corners of the lamp-lit room.

It was behavior he excelled at, reveled in. Behavior he couldn't indulge in because, hell, he was *married*. And finding his wife in this packed ballroom was like looking for a particular piece of hay in a haystack. Full-face masks were the norm and he hoped that Cal hadn't bothered with a wig. Her red hair would be a great way to identify her. Damn, he thought as he turned in a slow circle, he should've insisted on knowing exactly what she intended to wear.

But, in his defense, he was still amazed that he'd been able to carry on any type of conversation that morning on the deck. Cal's tiny barely there shirt and tight shorts just skimming the top of her thighs put his brain in neutral. He'd removed every type of lingerie imaginable—from silky negligees to crotchless panties—from a lot willing female bodies, and her plain, white pajamas hadn't been anything extraordinary. But her in them? *Dynamite.*

Quinn shook his head. This was *Cal* he was thinking about. *Stop it!*

You're only thinking about her, like that, Quinn rationalized, *because you're a red-blooded man and she was wearing next to nothing. And, because you haven't been laid for nearly six weeks, pretty much any woman will do. Even Cal. It's normal. It didn't mean anything.* He had a fake wife; their marriage was a con they were pulling on the world. Nothing between them would change.

Ever.

Quinn adjusted his mask and did another scan of the ballroom. With so many people here, he'd probably only find Cal after they were allowed to remove their masks around midnight. Quinn looked at his watch. Two and a half hours to go.

Hell.

He noticed a bar at the far end of the room and was about to head in that direction when he saw two of his favorite women standing to the left of him. Rory's mask barely covered her eyes and Brodie's huge stomach made identifying them easy.

Making his excuses, he walked over and quickly dropped a kiss on each of their cheeks and he briefly touched Brodie's pronounced baby bump.

"Ladies, you both are looking spectacular," he said, his compliment absolutely heartfelt. He genuinely liked the women his friends were in love with.

"How is my favorite girl?" he asked Rory.

Rory smiled, her eyes softening. Both she and Mac doted on their baby daughter, Rosie, as did they all. "She's fine, at home. Troy is babysitting."

"Good man, Troy," Quinn said, meaning it. He really liked Rory's best friend and the fact that a super-qualified nurse was looking after their precious Rosie

made them all feel more at ease. He turned to Brodie
and looked down at her bump.

"You look like you've swallowed a bowling ball,
Brodes."

"I feel like I've swallowed a bowling ball," Brodie replied, reaching up to touch his smooth jaw. She lifted his
mask and sighed before dropping the mask back onto
his face. "But let's talk about you, sexy guy. We didn't
recognize you until you spoke. Looking hot, Quinn. I
very much like the new look."

Oh, yeah, that. Cutting his hair and shaving off his
beard had been an impulsive decision. There was a salon
next to his dry cleaners and when he'd picked up his
tux, he'd popped his head in and saw that the place was
empty. He'd intended to trim his hair, shorten his beard,
but the stylist, who turned out to be young, pretty and
very persuasive, charmed him into going short. He'd
agreed, partly because she was cute but also because
everything else seemed to be changing in his life so he
thought he might as well change his looks too.

In for a penny and all that.

"What prompted the makeover?" Rory asked.

Quinn frowned at her. A makeover? He'd had a hair-
cut and shaved his beard off. Why was she busting his
chops? She'd obviously been hanging around Mac for
far too long. "It's *not* a makeover."

"It's a dramatic change—long hair to short and spiky,
no beard. When you end up looking ten times better—
which, I have to point out, should be illegal in your

case—it's a makeover." Rory started to lift his mask again, but Quinn gently pushed her hand away. "Those lips, that jaw."

"Those eyes," Brodie added.

Quinn felt the tips of his ears growing hot. He ran a finger around the edge of his collar. "Will you two stop? Please?" he begged.

"Yeah, please stop," Mac said as he joined them, his arms instantly going around Rory's waist. "I think I might gag."

"He just looks so different," Rory explained. "This new you is, well, hot." She fanned herself.

"Okay, honey, enough now," Mac said, an edge creeping into his voice.

Kade walked up to them with three glasses of champagne and ignored Brodie's dark look when he handed Rory and Kade a glass each and kept one for himself. "Hi, Quinn. Sorry, I didn't know you were here. I've ordered you a sparkling water, honey."

Brodie's frown deepened. "Oh, joy. Can I have a sip of champagne, at least?"

Quinn hid his smile as Kade monitored just how big a sip of alcohol Brodie was taking. When she went in for a second sip, Kade yanked the glass away. "That's enough."

Quinn smiled at Kade's protectiveness. His friends adored their women and Quinn was thrilled that they were so happy. Yet he also felt a little like a third wheel, a thought that would horrify them all. But it wasn't an unfamiliar feeling. In his parents' house he'd always felt on the outside looking in. Despite his ability to shoot the breeze, to charm blood out of a rock, or the panties off nuns, he'd seldom connected on an emotional level with people and shared very little of himself, even with his friends. Not because he didn't trust them—he did—it was just a habit he'd cultivated when he was a kid and one that still served him well.

He wasn't a talker, preferring to work his inner world out on his own. Cal was only the person he'd opened up to as a kid...

Quinn felt the energy in the room change, heard the low buzz of voices that indicated something was happening. He slowly turned and looked toward the door to see a woman walking into the ballroom.

Her dress left him—and every other male in the room—in no doubt as to how close to perfect her body was. If he could actually call what she was wearing a dress. The word *dress* implied fabric and there was little of that. It could only be designer and, like three quarters of the dresses in the room, it was black. Unlike the other dresses, it was ridiculously sexy.

The best way Quinn could think to describe it was that someone had painted her torso with fabric swirls. One started at her neck and covered a breast, while another ran under her arm and across her other breast and covered some of her stomach, meeting in a perfect point at her hip. A slit revealed a long, toned leg ending in a strappy, sky-high black-and-silver sandal.

Quinn forced his eyes up and took in the blunt-cut, chin-length, jet-black bob. He could see little of her face beneath the complex gold mask made from feathers, chains, beads and fake gemstones. Gorgeous skin, a pointed chin and lips painted a bright, siren, sexy red completed the picture.

She was exactly his type: sophisticated, sexy, mysterious. Hot enough to melt glass. Yet, she was missing…*something*.

Quinn looked at Mac and then at Kade, deeply amused that their mouths were open and that their eyes had glazed over. He watched, laughing quietly, as Brodie and Rory exchanged eye rolls.

He understood, intellectually, that she was the sexiest thing on two feet and, yeah, if he was single and acting like himself, he definitely would not say no if she suggested a little bed-based fun, but…

The memory of Cal, dressed in her simple white pajamas, sporting a messy head of red curls and sleepy, dark eyes, was infinitely more tempting and so much sexier than the smokin' body in a barely-there dress.

It was official—along with his long hair and his beard, he'd also lost his mind. No, Cal was *not* sexier than this babe. Cal was *not* sexy at all. She was his friend! Friends and sexy did *not* go together.

"I so need a drink," Quinn muttered. Or a brain transplant.

He barely felt Brodie's hand on his arm, didn't realize that she was trying to get his attention until her nails dug into his skin.

"I wanted to tell you how much I enjoyed meeting Callahan," Brodie said, her expression sincere. "She's so down-to-earth."

Oh, yeah, right. He remembered hearing something about Rory and Brodie inviting Cal to lunch last week. Quinn flicked another glance at the hot woman—she was definitely worth another look—before answering. "She always has been. Despite their wealth, her parents are too. Well, her dad is. Her mom passed away a long time ago."

"And you've known each other all your lives?" Rory asked.

Quinn nodded. "I met her when I was eight. She lived a few doors down from me. For the next decade I treated her home like mine."

Rory sipped her wine, interested. She looked around, made sure that no one outside the group could hear her question. "And there's never been anything between you?"

Quinn tossed his hands up, frustrated. "You've definitely been living with Mac for too long. We're friends. We've always been friends. Why does everyone keep asking that?"

Rory, the meddler, just smiled at his heated response. "Maybe, my darling Quinn, it's because it's a question that always gets a heated reaction from you."

"I *definitely* need a drink," Quinn growled. He

leaned forward and dropped his voice. "Fake marriage. Friends. Nothing has changed. Status quo. What else can I say to convince you? Should I go over and flirt with Miss Swirls over there to prove it to you?"

Quinn flicked a look across the room and noticed that her back was to him. That view was almost as luscious as the front, just acres of creamy skin from the base of her neck to low on her buttocks. Whoever designed that dress had to have a degree in engineering because Quinn hadn't the foggiest idea how it was attached to her body. When he went over to talk to her, to flirt with her—he was still allowed to flirt, wasn't he?—he'd try to work out how it all stayed tidy.

Kade's laugh rolled over him. "Sure, go ahead if that's what you want to do. But maybe, *possibly*, it's not *us* you're trying to convince."

Four

Her *husband* had stood her up, Cal realized, standing in the shadows on the terrace, taking a break from the busy ballroom. It was past eleven and she'd yet to find Quinn.

Okay, there were two hundred men at the bail, but it wasn't like Quinn, masked or not, would be hard to find. Long hair, heavy beard, taller and broader than most. She hoped he made an appearance by midnight. People would be expecting him to stand at her side when she thanked her guests for attending, when she called for their masks to be removed. If he wasn't, then there would be questions—questions neither of them needed, especially since the world seemed to be buying their fake marriage and the interest in their personal lives seemed to be waning.

From the shadows, Cal had an unrestricted view of the ballroom and she scanned the room, idly noticing that the dance floor was packed. Nope, couldn't see him... *Dammit, Rayne!*

She did another slow scan of the room, ostensibly to look for Quinn but knowing that she wouldn't mind taking another long look at the guy she'd been trading glances with all evening. She first noticed him early in the evening, soon after she arrived, and while she couldn't really make out his features—*damn these masks!*—she instinctively knew that he was six foot something of coiled power, radiating testosterone, heat and... God, sex.

Hot, messy, slow, dirty, *sexy* sex.

The kind of sex she'd never experienced since all her lovers had been more of the this-is-about-me-not-you type. And Toby had been their king.

Jerk...

Anyway, she was just so grateful that she felt sexually attracted to someone besides Quinn. That proved to her that her long dormant libido had come out of hibernation and she was attracted to good-looking men in general and not Quinn in particular. Her lust wasn't directed at Quinn specifically so that was a relief.

Such a relief.

Cal inhaled the gently fragranced night air. She'd escaped to the balcony partly because she needed a time-out but mostly because she'd felt Hot Guy's eyes on her at various times during the evening. It started with a prickle between her shoulder blades and then heat traveled from her coccyx up her spine and she knew that HG was looking at her, that he was the reason for the sudden bump of her heart, the fact that the air had disappeared from the room. She'd turn and, yeah, as she suspected, he'd been looking at her. Yet he never made a move to approach her; he'd just kept his brooding, intense gaze on her.

Animal magnetism—she suddenly understood that concept. Totally, absolutely, innately. It didn't matter that she hadn't seen his face, heard him speak—those details were inconsequential. All she knew was that she wanted to get her hands on that body, to explore that wide chest, those big shoulders, the muscles of those long, long legs.

Her attraction to him and, she supposed, to Quinn made her feel happy. The throb between her legs and the flutter in her stomach made her feel normal again. For the first time in Vancouver, in nearly a decade, she felt strong and confident and in control. During her marriage, events like this had felt like minefields and she'd tiptoed her way through the evening, fumbling her way to the end. She constantly monitored her words, checked her responses, made sure that nothing she did or said could cause offense.

Amazing what a few years and being Toby-free could do, Cal thought. She was wearing a dress that Toby would never have allowed her to wear, had slapped on siren-red lipstick that he would've hated and she'd spent the evening gently flirting with every man who'd approached her. She'd had *fun*.

Cal heard the beat from the band and as the vocalist belted out the first line of a new song, she shimmied her hips, lifting her shoulders in a sensuous roll.

Dancing alone, in the moonlight, Callahan?

She heard Toby's sneering voice in her head and smiled as she raised her arms over her head and did a slow, sexy, shimmery twirl.

Yep. It's my ball and I can dance if I want to...

Big hands landed on her waist and spun her around. She sucked in an astounded breath but didn't resist when Hot Guy walked backward, stopping when her back rested against the cool wall behind her.

Cal's eyes widened as his long form pushed her into the stone and blocked out all the light in this already dark corner. She could taste his breath—whiskey and peppermint—and her heart threatened to climb out of her chest. She should be scared, she thought, but she wasn't. She was just utterly, comprehensively turned on.

"You smell like wildflowers...*ah, crap*!"

God, she recognized that voice; she knew that voice as well as she knew her own. *"Quinn?"*

So Hot Guy was Quinn and her libido, dammit, was still only attracted to one guy, the *wrong* guy.

Quinn's curse flew over her head, but she didn't care. She didn't want to think about who he was, *what* he was.

His hands on her hips made her heart race; his thigh between her legs made her hot. She'd never wanted anyone's lips over hers as much as she wanted his, here on this terrace with four hundred people inside dancing and chatting.

The moment hung, heavy with expectation, vibrating with intensity. Caught up in passion and in the fantasy of the moment, she put her fingers on his lips and shook her head, not wanting the fantasy to evaporate.

They were both masked and they could pretend… God, she needed to pretend.

"Kiss me."

Cal couldn't see his expression beneath his mask and it was too dark to see the emotion in his eyes. She felt his hesitation and worried that he would back off, that he'd yank them back to reality, to their lives. When his mouth softened and his thumb drifted over her ribs, she knew that he was as tempted as she was, that she wasn't the only one wanting to visit Fantasy Land.

He finally ducked his head and his mouth hovered over hers, teasing, tempting. She waited, knowing he would get to it, in his own time. He wasn't a man who could be rushed and she didn't want him to. She wanted the anticipation, the headiness, the bubble, the fizz. She wanted it all.

Minutes, hours, eons later, he lowered his head and his mouth brushed hers. Her hands trembled as she pushed her fingers into his hair. His fingertips dug into the bare skin at her waist, and by their own volition her hands parted his jacket to touch the muscles at his waist, to echo his hold on her.

As he kissed her, as she lost herself in him, the world faded away, melting in the joy his mouth created. In this moment, as his mouth invaded hers, she wasn't the good girl, Cauley's daughter, the do-gooder with the sterling reputation. She wasn't the heiress, the widow, the fake wife, the princess.

She was Cal. Quinn holding her was all that was important. When they kissed, her world, for the first time in far too long, made sense. Here in this moment, there was perfect clarity, absolute understanding...of everything.

Then the universe shifted as he pushed his hips into hers, rocking his long erection into her stomach. Now his kisses weren't enough and she made a sound of desperation deep in her throat, groaning as his hand left her hip to cover her breast, his thumb finding her nipple and teasing it to a point that was almost painful. In response she dropped her hand and tried to encircle him, frustrated by the barrier of his pants.

Quinn murmured something, his words too low to make out, but she knew they were hot and encouraging so she fumbled for the zipper of his fly as he pushed away the clingy fabric covering her right breast to reveal her bare skin. Then his amazing lips sucked her bottom lip into his mouth and she stumbled on her heels, utterly off balance. A broad hand on her butt kept her upright and his other hand dipped into the slit high on her thigh, found the tiny triangle of her thong and pushed the silk aside. As he touched her intimately, knowingly, she found him, long and hot and jerking with need. She rubbed his tip and he stroked her clit and she started to free-fall…

"Please, please, please. Don't stop," she begged, arching her back as he pulled her nipple against the roof of his mouth. She needed him to push her over the edge, needed him to take her there…to that magical place that had always, always been just out of her reach. "That feels so damn amazing. God…"

It took Cal a little while to realize that he had, in fact, stopped, that he was statue-still, that his fingers had stopped creating magic and that his mouth had left her breast. It was a couple more seconds before it sank in that his fingers were leaving her body, that he'd—

That he'd stopped at a crucial point. He was going to leave her high and dry and throbbing with need.

What? Why? What had happened? Cal sucked in air, trying to get her bearings, trying to get her noodle-like knees to lock.

When she thought she could put words together, she looked up at him, adjusting her mask so she could see through the slit-like holes. "Why did you stop?"

"Because making love to my best friend up against a wall just outside a ballroom with her guests inside was never part of the freakin' deal!"

Twenty seconds ago he'd had Cal's nipple in his mouth, his fingers on her—oh, God, he couldn't go there. He'd been a minute away from pushing her dress up to her hips and sliding home. He'd been lost, in the best way possible, in the heat of her—deaf, dumb, blind and crazy with lust…

For Cal!

For his best friend!

Quinn stepped away from Cal, zipped up his pants and pulled his stupid mask from his face, throwing it onto the floor at their feet. He heard Cal's gasp and looked at her through narrowed eyes. She'd pushed her mask up into her wig and he saw desire blazing from her eyes.

He felt the jerk in his pants and closed his eyes. He still wanted her, still wanted to take the…the…*situation* to its natural conclusion. Judging by her rapid breathing and her squirming, so did she.

He was not about to take Callahan up against a wall. He wanted to, but he wouldn't.

And the frustrations just kept rolling in, Quinn thought, pushing his fingers through his short hair. He walked away to grip the edge of the balcony, trying to get his labored breathing under control. He was only out here because he was annoyed at not finding Callahan in the ballroom, frustrated because he wanted to see her, talk to her, laugh with her.

Bothered because his thoughts kept wandering to his fake wife, and wondering where she was, he'd deliberately turned his attention to Swirls and, admittedly, that hadn't been a hardship. He'd hoped that she'd distract him from his current obsession with his fake wife.

She hadn't, so, needing a break from the perfume-scented air inside, he'd wandered onto the balcony. When he saw Swirls swaying in the moonlight, he'd stepped up to her, thinking he'd dance with her, needing distraction from the bubbling sexual tension and frustration living with Red caused.

Then all hell broke loose…

"You shaved your beard, cut your hair," Cal whispered, her fingers against her mouth. "I didn't recognize you."

Quinn placed his hands behind his head and stomped down the terrace, staring into space. He didn't like feeling so off balance so he took refuge in an emotion he did understand: angry frustration. He spun around and glared at her. "So you allowed a stranger to put his hands on you? Do you know how dangerous that is? God, I could've been anyone! A predator! A rapist!"

Cal's mouth fell open. "Are you seriously lecturing me? Right now?"

Quinn was about to respond when he realized that her right breast—her perfect, perfect breast—was still on show, the fabric of her dress pulled to the side. He dropped his hands and waved his hand in the general direction of her torso. "Will you please cover up?"

Cal looked down and gasped. She hastily pulled the fabric back in place and he almost groaned in disappointment.

"You don't need to be such a jerk," Cal muttered.

"You don't need to be so damn tempting," Quinn retorted without thinking. He closed his eyes and tipped his head back, praying for sanity. Or a lightning strike. Or a time machine to roll them back to an hour ago, to earlier in the evening, to birth.

Except that he couldn't quite regret kissing Callahan. Kissing Cal had been…man, so wonderful. Even worse was the fact that he wanted to do it again, and so much more. God, he was in trouble.

"Let's take a couple of breaths and calm down." Quinn rolled his head in order to release the knots of tension in his neck and when he felt marginally calmer, he spoke again.

"Look, Red—" he deliberately used his childhood nickname for her "—the fact remains that you're you and this was…wrong."

Well, not wrong per se but wrong for them. They were best friends. He didn't want to lose her. Lose that.

"Wrong?"

Quinn ran a finger around the edge of his collar and wondered where all the air had gone. Damn, if this was anyone else, he'd have managed to charm his way out of this situation, but she wasn't a stranger and he was living with her, *married to her.* Fake married but still…

"Well, not wrong but…weird."

"Weird?"

Why did she keep throwing his words back in his face?

Quinn shook his head and prayed for patience. He was trying to think, dammit! But his brain refused to work properly because it was still processing how Cal felt, tasted…

He took a step forward, wanting to kiss her again and abruptly stopped. Closing his eyes, Quinn told his libido that finishing what they'd started would be a very bad idea.

Very, very crazy-bad idea.

Sleeping with her would be the equivalent of dousing the friendship bridge with napalm before igniting it with a surface-to-missile rocket.

Best friend, living together, fake wife. The complications were crazy.

He needed to fix this, now, immediately. And to do that he'd have to stay calm—and keep his hands off her—because the situation was amped enough without any more drama.

He needed a joke. He and Cal had always been able to laugh together. It would be a way to lighten the mood.

Except that he couldn't think of anything remotely funny to say. And God, this silence was becoming even more awkward. And tense. And…hot. Cal gnawed her bottom lip and placed her hand behind her back and inadvertently lifted her chest and he wished that she hadn't covered up.

Okay, he *had* to get them back on track. "Look, I don't want this to cause awkwardness between us."

"I think we are way beyond awkward, Quinn."

"I'm sorry." It was all he could think of to say.

Cal drilled him with an intense look. "What, exactly, are you sorry for?"

Quinn covered his eyes with a hand and rubbed his eyes. "Why can't you see that I'm just trying to not make the biggest mistake of my life, Cal?"

He dropped his hand, blinked and his heart felt like it was in free fall as he waited for her response. And when she spoke again, she sliced his heart in two. "Of all the mistakes you've made, and you've got to admit that there have been some zingers, I'm devastated that you think that almost making love to me was your biggest."

Quinn watched Cal walk away and wished he could find the words to explain that his friendship with her was, possibly, the only thing he'd ever done right. That was the reason why making love to her would be such a mistake. He couldn't risk losing the best, purest relationship he had in his life for a quick orgasm.

Orgasms were easy to find; somebody who understood him wasn't.

Cal kept a healthy distance between her and Quinn as they walked down the dock toward his yacht. Cal looked to her left and saw that Quinn was staring straight ahead, his jaw tight.

They hadn't exchanged a word since leaving the ballroom and the silence between them was heavy and saturated with tension. They'd had their fights before— all friends did—but this situation wasn't that simple.

It wasn't simple at all.

She'd had her hand around his... Cal lifted her hands and rubbed them over her face, no longer concerned about dislodging her wig or smearing her makeup. She'd had her hand in his pants...

Cal shivered again and this time it wasn't from humiliation; it was because she wanted to touch him again. That and more. She wanted to kiss him, needed to feel his mouth on her breasts, needed to feel that pulsing build between her legs. She wanted him to take her over the edge, to make her scream as he filled her, stretched her.

Cal groaned and stumbled. Quinn grabbed her bare elbow and his fingers dug into her skin and Cal just managed to keep her frustrated moan behind her teeth. She stopped walking and stared at the ground, not wanting him to see her face because if he did, he would know how much she still wanted him, how close she was to begging—*begging!*—him to finish what he started.

"Are you okay?" Quinn, asked, his voice low.

Cal nodded, conscious that his hand was still holding her arm and sending sparks through her. "Fine."

"You're cold." Quinn placed his hands on her bare upper arms and rubbed her skin and Cal had to stop herself from purring. "Where is your coat?"

She had no idea. In his car? At the ball? Who knew? "Uh…"

Quinn shrugged out of his tuxedo jacket and draped it around her shoulders. Cal pulled her wig off, handed it to Quinn and pushed her arms into the sleeves of his jacket, still warm from his body. His scent—sandal-wood and citrus—mingled with the smell of the sea and she felt that buzz in her womb again, was conscious of the beat of butterfly wings in her stomach. God, she was definitely going off the deep end.

She heard Quinn's heavy sigh. "Let's get home, Red. It's been a hell of an evening."

It really had. Cal folded her arms across her chest, bunching the fabric of his beautifully tailored, designer jacket. They continued in silence, climbed the steps to the main deck and Cal waited while Quinn unlocked the sliding doors and flipped on some lights. She stepped inside and shrugged off her shoes. She slipped off his jacket and handed it to him, aware that his eyes seemed to be taking a long time to move off her chest. She looked down and was thankful to see that everything was properly covered up.

But Quinn still seemed fascinated by her dress.

"That dress. It's a damned miracle I can string a sentence together," Quinn drawled, his eyes hot but his expression rueful as he dropped his jacket on top of her mask and wig. "There were more than a few eyebrows raised when your guests realized that you were behind that getup."

"I assumed there would be," Cal told him, heading for the kitchen. Leaving the lights off, she opened the fridge and pulled out a bottle of water and lifted it up in a silent offer. Quinn nodded and she pulled out another one, handed it to him. Quinn, always a gentleman, cracked the lid, handed the bottle back to her before opening his own. Cal sipped and looked at the inky water outside, lights from skyscrapers behind them tossing golden ribbons across the water.

"Want to explain that?" Quinn asked, taking a seat across the island from her, his elbows on the granite.

In the light spilling from a lamp she took her first long look at Quinn, clean-shaven and sexy. His beard was no longer a distraction; she could see the line of his strong jaw, the smooth skin of his neck, the tiny dimple in his right cheek, the scar on his top lip. She'd given him that scar, she remembered. She'd smacked him with a metal photo frame for dismembering four of her favorite Barbie dolls.

It had taken three weeks for her to talk to him again. At seven, she'd been more stubborn than most.

"By the way, I like seeing your face." She tipped her head. "But you'd look better with some stubble."

That was the type of comment Cal-his-friend would make, the Cal she was trying to be.

Quinn ran his hand over his smooth jaw. "Thanks. It's a change. And why do I suspect that you are trying to change the subject?"

Cal sighed. She'd forgotten that Quinn wasn't that easily distracted. "Back to my dress, huh?"

"Would you prefer to talk about what happened on the terrace?" Quinn asked, his voice low but resolute.

Cal scrunched her nose. "No," she admitted. She

wanted to do it again, but she most certainly did not want to talk about it.

"Then back to the dress," Quinn told her, looking determined. And remote and nothing like the crazy-with-need man who'd kissed her with such skill on the terrace. Where had he gone? She'd like him back.

"Though we will have to discuss what happened between us at some point."

"Does never work for you?" Cal asked, feeling the heat rise up her neck.

Quinn just sent her a steady look and her shoulders slumped.

"You were never very good at being an ostrich," Cal complained. "Sometimes you've just got to shove your head in the sand and wait for the storm to pass over."

"Not the way I work, Red," Quinn said. "So, your dress. I think you wore it to make a statement."

"And what statement might that be?" Cal demanded.

He was perceptive and so damn smart. Oh, she knew he didn't think so; he'd been compared to his brilliant brothers all his life and that made him think that he was less than. Unlike them, he wasn't a genius, but he had something his brothers didn't: the ability to read people, to look below the surface and work out what made people tick. Quinn was intelligent, but, more than that, he was street-smart.

"Your dress was a declaration of independence, a way to tell the world that you are your own person, fully adult and fully responsible. That you are, finally, making your own choices."

Yeah, *that*. Her dress had also been a silent way for her to send a message to Toby's world that she wasn't the polite, meek pushover she once was. It was her act of rebellion, years overdue, and she didn't regret her choice.

Dancing in the dark, allowing a stranger to put his hands on her, had been another little rebellion, her way to walk on the wild side. Except that the stranger wasn't a stranger...

Cal placed her elbows on the cool granite of the island and massaged her temples with the tips of her fingers. Why couldn't she stop thinking about his lips on hers, the way he tasted—sexy, dark, sinful?

"God, Cal, don't look at me like that," Quinn begged, his fists clenched at his sides. "This is hard enough as it is."

"I've never been attracted to you in my life. Why now?" Cal moaned.

"I'm choosing to believe that it was because it was a masked ball and because everyone is encouraged to misbehave," Quinn replied, his voice sounding strangled.

Cal lifted her head and met his eyes. "So if I walk around the island and kiss you, you're going to push me away and tell me that the attraction only lasted as long as we were masked and in the dark?"

Quinn stared at her and she saw the thin line of his lips, watched his eyes narrow. She knew that he was considering whether to lie to her, to tell her exactly that.

He opened his mouth and the lie hovered between them, silent but powerful. Then his shoulders slumped and he rubbed his big hand over his face.

"I want to say that," he admitted, his voice rough. "But I've never lied to you and I won't start now."

"And?"

Quinn stared up at the ceiling. "I want you, but I don't want to want you. So what are we going to do about this, Callahan?"

Well, frankly, she'd like to get naked and hit the nearest horizontal surface and let him rocket her to an orgasm. She'd been so close on the terrace and she still felt unsettled, grumpy... She sighed. Unfulfilled. Horny.

Cal wanted to suggest one night—one crazy, hot, steamy, uninhibited night of passion. They had a few hours until the sun came up, before life intruded and they could spend that time exploring their attraction, giving and taking pleasure. They could step out of their friendship and pretend the past and the future didn't exist, live entirely for the moment. Wasn't that what you were supposed to do? Carpe diem and all that? The past was gone and the future was still on its way...

They could start off with her sitting on this island and then they could move onto that blocky couch. After that they could shower together; she'd seen his massive shower—all sorts of things could happen in that over-sized space. Then they could nap before he woke her up for round three, or four...

"I think we should go to bed, separately, and get our heads on straight. Forget this ever happened."

Cal's eyebrows slowly pulled together as she made sense of his words. That sounded suspiciously like she wasn't going to get lucky. Not tonight or anytime soon. There would be no couch or shower or nakedness and definitely no orgasms.

Forget this happened? How was she supposed to do that? He'd had his hand between her legs, for God's sake!

"Sex is easy, Cal. Friendship is not. I'm not tossing a lifetime of memories away because we want to scratch an itch. This stops here, tonight. We are friends and we are not going to color outside the lines."

Cal blinked. She definitely wasn't getting lucky tonight, dammit.

"Uh…okay?" It definitely wasn't okay! There was nothing remotely okay about this stupid situation!

"We're going to forget this ever happened. We're going to wake up tomorrow morning and we're going back to being friends, easy with each other, the way we've been for the last twenty years. Clear?"

Cal glared at him. "Stop being bossy. I heard you the first time. You don't want me and we're going back to being friends."

"I never said I didn't want you!" Quinn threw up his hands and climbed off his stool, slapping his hands on his waist before dropping his head to stare at the floor. He always did that when he thought that his temper was slipping away, when he felt like he was losing control of the situation. Good, she wanted him to lose control. She wanted his reassurance that she wasn't the only one whose world had been rocked by their kiss, by the passion that had flared—unexpectedly but white-hot—between them.

"Go to bed, Cal," Quinn said. "Please. I don't want us to do something we'll regret. Sex has a way of changing everything, of complicating lives. My life is complicated enough and I'm trying to do the right thing here. Please, I'm begging you, go to bed."

Her libido, long neglected, whimpered in protest, but her brain, slowly regaining control, insisted that he was right, that she had to be sensible. Cal pursed her lips, hitched up her skirt and walked away. Being sensible, she decided, was no fun at all.

Five

Quinn watched Callahan run down the stairs to the lower deck and when he heard her bedroom door slam shut, he grabbed his jacket and slipped into the night. He walked to the promenade, the popular walkway empty at this late hour. Most of the boats were dark, he noticed as he shoved his hands into the pockets of his pants. Ignoring the bite of the wind and the mist brushing his face with wet fingers, he walked to the nearest pier. At the end of the pier he rested his arms on the railing and took a deep breath of the cold, briny air. Three in the morning, the loneliest, most honest hour of the day, he thought.

Situation report, Quinn decided. He'd friend-zoned Callahan. He'd said no to some hot, bedroom-based fun with the woman he liked best in the world. He was as proud of himself as he was pissed off. Was he out of his mind? Or was he, for once, thinking with his big brain?

A little of both, he admitted, staring at the awesome views of the Vancouver skyline. He had the same views from his yacht, but because he didn't trust himself not to run down to her room and sneak into bed with her and lose himself in the wonder that was Callahan, he was standing on a dock freezing his ass off instead.

Resigned to the fact that he was going to be cold for a little while still, Quinn watched the lights reflecting off the water and tried to make sense of the evening, trying not to imagine how it would feel to explore that luscious mouth, how she would look after he peeled that sinful dress off her equally sinful body...

Quinn's groan bounced off the water and he gripped the railing, dropping his head between his taut arms. He couldn't, shouldn't, wouldn't. Apart from what he had with Mac and Kade, his friendship with Callahan was the only relationship in his life that was pure, uncomplicated, based entirely on who he was as a person and not on who people expected him to be.

The rest of the world saw the pieces of him he allowed them to see. Depending on whom he was with, he could be the charming rogue, the life and soul of the party, the daredevil adventurer, the tough and focused coach.

Cal saw the big picture of who he was and he, in turn, knew what made her tick, understood what drove her. Well, he had up until she got engaged to her now-dead husband.

Quinn's hands tightened on the railing. He still had no idea why she'd married Carter and why she still, to this day, refused to discuss him. Carter was firmly off-limits and Quinn wondered why. It wasn't like Cal to keep things to herself.

Then again, Carter had always been a touchy subject between them. From the first moment Quinn heard she was dating the forty-year-old businessman, he'd mishandled his reaction. He'd told her, in fairly salty language, that Carter was an idiot and that she needed to have her head examined. Cal had told him to keep his opinions to himself. He'd tried, but when they announced their engagement, he'd told her, stupidly, that he wouldn't watch her throw her life away and that if she married Carter, he was walking out of her life. In his youth and arrogance he'd thought that nothing could come between them, that their friendship was that solid, that important.

She'd married Carter anyway.

Carter, her marriage and his death were still taboo subjects. Was it because the pain ran too deep? Because Carter was—God forbid—her one true love, someone who couldn't be replaced? Quinn hoped not. Unlike him, she wasn't cut out to be alone, to flit from casual affair to casual affair, from bed to bed.

Hearing that it was extremely unlikely that he'd ever be able to father a child—amazing what routine blood tests could kick up!—just cemented his resolve to be alone, to choose when and how he interacted with people, with women. He'd trained himself not to think about what he couldn't have—a wife, a family—and he'd never allowed himself to take a relationship further than a brief affair. What was the point? It couldn't go anywhere...

But being attracted to someone who knew him so well scared him.

Cal was an essential part of his ragtag, cobbled-together family and you did not mess with family. She was his best friend and you did not try and play games with something that had worked so well for so long. You did not break what worked...

It did not matter if she had a body to die for and a mouth made for sin. It didn't matter that their kiss had been hotter than hell, that he'd been rocked to the soles of his feet. That he'd never felt so...

Quinn closed his eyes. He'd never felt so out of touch with himself, so caught up in the moment. A bomb could've dropped next to him and he wouldn't have noticed and that...well...freaked him out. Callahan—dark eyes and a steaming-hot body, the only woman he'd ever kissed who made him forget who he was, who made the world recede, caused his brain to shut down as soon as their lips met—was an impulse he could not act on, a risk he could not take. Because he could not, *would not* mess with the only family he had...especially when he'd never been part of the one he'd originally been given and he was unable to create his own.

Fact number one: Quinn was a good-looking guy.

Fact number two: he was a superbly talented kisser.

Fact number three: he was her best friend.

Fact number four: she'd acted like an idiot last night. Worse, she'd acted like a desperate puckbunny who'd throw her mother under a bus to get it on with a Maverick.

She was mortified.

Cal wiped the perspiration off her face with the back off her wrist and waited for her heart rate to drop. She'd pushed herself jogging this morning, trying to outrun her embarrassment. It hadn't worked. Now she had to face the music. Frankly, she'd rather have her eyes pecked out by a starving vulture.

If she was really, really lucky, then Quinn would've left the yacht already to do whatever he did on Saturday mornings and she could delay the inevitable for twelve or fourteen hours or so.

Cal heard the hiss of the coffeemaker, the bang of a cupboard door and realized that bitch Luck was laughing at her. Maybe if Cal slipped her trainers off, she could sneak past him…

Cal sighed. Running away from a situation—or running into another situation because she was running away from another—was how she made things worse. She was a grown-up, and she faced life head-on. She took responsibility for her actions, for her choices, for her life.

But she just didn't want to, not this morning. Cal lifted her foot to take off her trainers.

"Avoiding me, Red?"

Busted. Cal stared down at her multicolored trainers and eventually lifted her eyes to meet his. He was wearing his inscrutable mask, but his eyes expressed his wariness and more than a little confusion.

"Morning. How did you sleep?" Cal asked with false cheeriness.

Quinn lifted one mocking eyebrow. "About as well as you did."

Which would be not at all. If she had the same blue stripes under her eyes as Quinn did, then there wasn't enough makeup in the world that could do damage control.

"Coffee?" Quinn asked.

"Please."

Cal walked over to the window and placed her hand on the glass, looking at the low, gray clouds. The wind whipped up little peaks of white on the waves and, under her feet, the yacht rocked. She longed for a day of pure sunshine and she felt a sudden longing for a clear, hot day in Africa, the sun beating down on her shoulders, the shocking blue sky.

Quinn cleared his throat and she turned to see him holding out a mug. Cal took it and her eyes widened when a zing of pleasure shot through her as their fingers connected.

Their attraction hadn't dissipated in the cold light of morning.

Dammit.

Quinn leaned his shoulder into the glass and stared broodingly out of the window, his mouth a grim line. "We have a problem."

Of course they did.

Cal took a large sip of coffee before wrapping her hands around the mug. "What now?"

Quinn gestured to his tablet on the island. "Your dress caused a stir with the press."

Oh, that. Cal looked at the large clock on the wall behind him. "I haven't even had breakfast yet and you've been online already?"

Quinn snorted. "As if. No, Wren emailed me the highlights. That woman is a machine."

"I'd say," Cal replied. "So, what are they saying about my dress?"

"A lot. Some columnists said it was good to see you pushing the envelope. Others said it was too much. One suggested it was a dress more suited for a…" Quinn's words trailed off and he looked uncomfortable.

Ah, she'd expected that too. "A hooker?"

"A high-class one," Quinn clarified.

Like that made a difference.

"It was on the Celeb Chaser blog. Don't read the article—it was vicious."

"Give me the highlights," Cal demanded, her coffee sloshing in her stomach.

"You looked like a slut. Carter would be so embarrassed to see you like that. You're a disgrace to his name." Quinn scowled. "It also mentioned your dress is the first indication that my dissolute lifestyle is rubbing off on you."

Come on, how could anyone be rude enough to write that? "Moron," Cal stated, rolling her eyes.

"I'll get my lawyers to demand they write a retraction," Quinn told her, his lips thin with displeasure.

"I appreciate the gesture, but it's not worth the time or the effort," Cal said. "Were you embarrassed by what I wore?"

She didn't give a damn about Toby and his opinions—being dead, he had no say in anything she did or thought anymore. But she did care what Quinn thought. She'd always trusted his judgment. Had she gone a little overboard in an effort to assert her independence?

Quinn looked puzzled. "Are you really asking me if I was embarrassed to be seen with you wearing that dress?"

Well, yes. Cal nodded, hesitant.

"Why the hell would I be? Yeah, it was—let's call it minimalist—but you looked incredibly sexy." Quinn's mouth tipped up at the corners. "Hence me kissing the hell out of you on the terrace. I just wanted to get you out of it."

Cal waved his words away. "Okay, I get that, but

was it too much?' She took a deep breath. "Did I look, well, tarty?"

Quinn's smile was a delicious mixture of reassurance and male appreciation. "Red, you don't have a tarty bone in your body. You are all class, no matter what you wear."

Something hot and wicked arced between them and Cal found herself looking at his mouth, licking her lips. His eyes turned a deeper green, heated by desire, and she knew he was mentally stripping her, his hands on her skin, his mouth tasting her. God, she wanted him. Quinn broke their stare and she heard his long, frustrated sigh.

"Something else caught the press's attention last night," Quinn said. His worried voice broke the tense, sexually charged silence between them.

In the past eight hours, she'd kissed and groped her best friend and they'd upset the apple cart that was their relationship. She'd had no sleep and she wasn't sure how much more she could take.

Cal hauled in a deep breath and rolled her hand. "Hit me."

"Some reports are questioning whether there is trouble in paradise."

"Our paradise? Meaning our marriage?" Cal clarified. Of course there was trouble in paradise but nobody should realize that but them. "Did they catch us groping on the terrace?"

"There's nothing too unusual about a man and wife

getting hot and heavy, Callahan. If anything, that would've reinforced the fact that we are crazy about each other."

Oh. True. Cal wrinkled her nose, puzzled. "Then what?"

"I didn't join you on the stage when you gave your thank-you speech. When you told the guests that they could take their masks off, I was, apparently, scowling at you and looking less than happy. And we didn't dance and weren't as affectionate as we usually are toward each other."

Cal thought back and realized the reporters were right. She and Quinn usually had no problem touching each other. They'd always been affectionate. It meant nothing for her to hold his hand, for him to put his arm around her waist, to tuck her into his side. They enjoyed each other's company and the world noticed that. Toby had certainly noticed and he'd loathed her friendship with Quinn.

Last night, she and Quinn—after leaving the terrace with the memory of what they'd done fresh in their minds—hadn't known how to act around each other. She'd been both angry and turned on, both discombobulated and annoyed, and she knew Quinn well enough to know that, behind his cool facade, he was as unsettled as she was. The easiest course of action—the only way to get through the rest of the evening—was to ignore each other, to pretend they hadn't just tried to swallow each other whole.

"We have no choice but to ride the storm. And, according to Wren, that means arranging another outing to show the world that we are happy and in love and that all is well with our world," Quinn stated quietly.

A raindrop hit the window and Cal watched it run down the glass. "Except it's not."

"Yeah, but nobody knows that but us," Quinn stated. "We have to do this, Cal. We can't back out now."

She had to ask, she had to find out where they stood. "And what about last night? What do we do about what happened on the terrace?"

"That," Quinn said behind gritted teeth. "Now *that* we are going to simply ignore."

Quinn sat on the corner of Wren's desk, picked up her pen and twisted it through his fingers as Wren typed. After five minutes, she leaned back in her chair and crossed her legs.

"They can take potshots at me, Wren, but saying that Cal looked like a hooker is not, and never will be, acceptable," Quinn stated, still fuming despite the fact that it was Monday and he'd had the weekend to work through his anger. "I want them to write a retraction or else I will sue them for libel."

Wren placed her hand on his knee and gave it a reassuring squeeze. "Hon, you know that won't work and that it will just add fuel to the fire. Let it go."

He couldn't. He'd seen the worry in Cal's eyes when she'd asked him whether her dress had been inappropriate, had seen that she was questioning her taste, her own judgment. He was so angry that one article—two hundred badly written words—had caused her to question herself.

"Trust me, there's nothing you can do and you reacting to it is exactly what they want you to do." Wren patted his knee again.

Quinn knew she was right and that still irritated the hell out of him. He wasn't the type to walk away. He always preferred action to negotiation, doing to thinking. "Do you know who this Celeb Chaser is?" he asked, still not ready to let it go.

Wren didn't answer him. "Do you want what's best for Cal?" she demanded, her feminine face turning tough.

What kind of question was that? She knew he did.

"Not responding, in any way, to this article is what's best for Cal," Wren told him. "And that's not negotiable."

Wren just cocked her head when his curse bounced off the wall. Quinn swiped his palm across his face and sent her an apologetic look. "Sorry. Frustrated."

"Sure you are, but I don't think it's the article that's the true source of your frustration."

When he didn't ask her what she was implying, Wren shrugged. "So, I made reservations at Sylvie's for eight tonight for you and Cal. After Sylvie's, you are going dancing at Beat. Try to look like you are having fun, like you are in love. We need the press to believe that."

Beat? He'd never heard of it and he thought he knew all of the trendiest clubs in the city. "Is that the new club we invested in, the one in Sandy Cove?"

Wren shook her head. "That's Cue, as in billiards. No, Beat isn't a club. I suppose it's more of an old-fashioned dance hall, sexy music, low lighting… It's very romantic."

Yay, romance. Exactly what they needed because they weren't sexually frustrated enough already.

Oh, this just got better and better. Quinn rubbed the back of his neck. He understood Wren's need to do some damage control after the ball—he and Cal had looked like anything but the newly married, blissfully happy couple they were supposed to be—but was a romantic dinner and dancing really necessary? Surely they could just hit a club, let the press take a couple of photos of them looking happy and the balance of the universe would be restored. If they went to a club, then they wouldn't have to talk much and that could only be a good thing because talking to Cal had suddenly become hard work.

For twenty-plus years conversation had flowed between them easily. One kiss and a hot grope and they were tongue-tied, desperately awkward.

He hated it. They needed to resolve it, and quickly. He couldn't imagine going through the rest of his life, this marriage, this *week* not being able to talk to Cal. Cal was his sounding board, his moral compass, his reality check. Although she was living in his house, it felt like she was back in Africa and they had no means to communicate.

And when he wasn't thinking about all the things he wanted to discuss with her, then he was thinking about their kiss, the way she tasted, the softness and scent of her endlessly creamy skin. He wanted to kiss every freckle on her face, wanted to see if her ridiculously long eyelashes could tickle his cheek, how her hands felt wrapped around his...

"You two need to look like you're in love. Sylvie's is romantic and Beat is a sexy, sexy place." Wren's cool voice interrupted his little fantasy.

"I've given a few of my more trustworthy press contacts the details. They'll be there to snap you looking hot and happy. Do not mess it up," she warned, drilling a finger into his thigh.

"Why do you automatically assume that I'm the one who'll muck it up?" Quinn grumbled.

"The best predictor of future behavior is past behavior," Wren replied, her voice tart. "You threw the first punch in that bar two years ago. You BASE jumped off that building and got arrested for trespassing because you had no right to be there. You were caught flying down the highway on your Ducati. You—"

Quinn held up his hand. "Okay, point made. I will be a good boy and act like a besotted fool."

Wren cocked her head and frowned at him. "Is that what you think love is? Foolish?"

Quinn looked at her, caught off guard by her question. "Sorry?"

"I'm just curious as to why you think that love is foolish. You make it sound like a waste of time, like it's boring, almost annoying."

"You get all that from one word?" Quinn lifted an eyebrow, hoping that his expression would dissuade her from pursuing the subject. Unfortunately Wren wasn't, and never had been, intimidated by him.

"The definition of *foolish* is *lacking good sense or judgment*. Pretty fitting coming from the man who has sold a million papers thanks to his lack of judgment. I find it interesting that you'll take physical risks but you won't risk your heart. That you think bailing off a building with just a parachute to break your fall is acceptable but falling in love is dangerous."

"I never said it was dangerous. I said it was foolish."

Wren snorted. "Because it's dangerous. Because your heart could get hurt."

"This is a ridiculous conversation," Quinn muttered, standing up. "And it's over. Will you email Cal the details about tonight or should I?"

"It's your date. You do it." Wren crossed her legs and smiled. "Feeling a bit hot under the collar because I mentioned love, Rayne? It's not so bad, you know—your buds seem to be stupidly happy as they go about creating their families."

Creating their families... Quinn hauled in a deep breath, hoping the air would blow away his resentment.

He couldn't have what everyone else did—not in the way they had it—and he was trying to do the best he could with what he did have. Why couldn't anyone see that?

Ah, maybe because you've never told a soul about what you're missing?

"Are you done?" he asked Wren, his voice tight with annoyance.

"I just want you to be happy, Quinn," Wren told him, her voice soft but sincere.

Quinn stood up and jammed his hands into the back pockets of his jeans. "The thing is, Wren, I am happy."

"Could've fooled me," Wren muttered as he left the room.

Six

Sylvie's was a luxurious, upmarket restaurant serving traditional Italian cuisine in the fashionable Gastown area of Vancouver. It had been a while since she'd eaten at the award-winning restaurant and on any other night she would be looking forward to the evening in the steel-and-glass, exposed-brick restaurant with its incredible wine selection and innovative dishes.

Before the ball, Quinn would've been her favorite person to dine with. They would spend ages discussing the menu and deciding what they would eat, arguing about who ordered what because they would, inevitably, end up swapping dishes halfway through. Or she would eat a third of her meal and Quinn would polish off the rest. But that would be dining with the old Quinn, her best friend, not the Quinn who'd pinned her to a wall and kissed the hell out of her, who'd stroked her to the point of overheating and then backed away.

The Quinn she still wanted and couldn't have.

Cal, dressed in a thong and a tiny strapless bra, glared at her bed and the pile of clothes she'd tossed onto it. What was she supposed to wear on a date that wasn't a date with a husband who wasn't actually a husband, with a man who was your best friend but whom you really wanted to get naked with?

Did that make any sense at all?

Cal placed her hand behind her head and groaned. Should she wear the fire-red shift dress with cowboy boots for a country-chic look? Or should she pair it with heels for an urban-chic look? But the long sleeves might be too hot for dancing. Designer jeans and a bustier? Nah, too sexy. Maybe the halter-neck, vintage 1950s, black-and-white, floral dress with her cherry-red stilettos? She had to make up her mind sometime soon— Quinn would be knocking on her door and she still had to do her makeup and her hair.

All she wanted to do was pull on a pair of yoga shorts, her Feed Me Ice Cream T-shirt and veg in front of the TV, eating pizza and drinking red wine. She wanted to watch a horror movie with Quinn, both of them mocking the special effects and providing commentary throughout. She wanted to put her head on his shoulder, or her feet in his lap, have him swipe the half-eaten piece of pizza from her hand.

She wanted him to pick her up and lay her on her back, lean over her and slide his mouth over hers, have his hand drift up her waist and encounter her breast, his thumb swiping her nipple. Cal closed her eyes, imagining him pushing her pants over her hips, exposing her to his hot gaze. His finger sliding over her, testing her, groaning when he realized she wanted him as much as he wanted her...

"Red, have you seen my wallet?"

Cal's head snapped up as her door opened. It took her a moment to realize the object of her fantasies was standing in her doorway, athletic shorts riding low on his hips, his broad chest glistening with perspiration. He'd been for a run, Cal remembered. They'd passed each other on the dock as she'd arrived home. He'd been wearing a shirt then and hadn't bothered to talk to her except to snap out a brief "See you soon."

Cal bit her bottom lip, her eyes traveling over those long, muscled, hair-roughened thighs; up and over that ridiculously defined abdominal pack; across his broad chest. God, he was hot. When she reached his face, she realized his eyes were still south of the border. Cal lifted her hand to touch her chest and encountered the soft lace of her strapless bra, the warmth of her breast spilling over the top.

She wasn't exactly wearing much, just a brief pair of panties that matched her bra. And Quinn seemed to like what he was looking at. Should she pick up her dress and cover herself or just stand there? Before their kiss, before the madness, she would've mocked him, told him that he looked like a goldfish with his open mouth and sent him on his way.

The only place she wanted to send him was into her bed, to get naked under her covers.

God, she was in so much trouble.

Cal watched as Quinn placed his hands on his hips and closed his eyes. Her eyes looked south again and, yes, there was a ridge in his pants that hadn't been there before. "God. This, you…"

Cal cocked her head, intrigued. Quinn was never disconcerted, was never at a loss for words. He always had a witty comeback, a way to diffuse tension, a smart-aleck comment. Right now he looked as flustered and, judging by the steel pipe in his pants, as turned on as she was.

"Uh… I'll find my wallet and I'll see you downstairs."

Cal released the breath she was holding as he spun around and walked away. She forced her legs to move across the pale floor to shut the door he'd left open.

When she'd proposed this marriage, she'd thought Quinn to be a safe bet, someone who wouldn't disturb her calm, orderly life. How could she have been so wrong? He was supposed to be the one man in her life, the one relationship that was stable, solid and unchangeable. Platonic, dammit.

She'd never believed that she would spend her nights—and a good part of her days—flipping between imagining what making love to Quinn would feel like and reminding herself that sleeping with Quinn would not be a good idea.

Having sex with Quinn would make their situation even more complicated; it would be another layer to disassemble when they split up. They were risking their friendship, something that was incredibly important to both of them.

When she felt brave enough to be very honest, she knew she was also terrified that if she slept with Quinn, she could open the portal to feeling something deeper and more intense than she did right now. Those emotions had the potential to be too powerful and if she surrendered to them, she felt like she was granting someone else—Quinn—control over her heart, her life.

She couldn't do that, not again. Not ever. No one would have control over her again.

Until something changed, until they managed to navigate their way back to friendship, they were caught in sexual purgatory, Cal realized. Unable to be lovers but definitely more than friends. It was, she noted, a very short walk from purgatory to hell.

"Let's talk about us sleeping together."

Cal had been concentrating on her *fritto misto di mare*, thinking that the food at Sylvie's was utterly delightful, when Quinn dropped his bombshell statement. She swallowed her half-chewed prawn, washed it down with a sip of fruity white wine and leaned back in her chair. Quinn carried on eating, slicing into his roasted monk fish and lifting his fork to his mouth. He chewed, looked pensive and went back to his dish to prepare another bite.

"After an hour of laborious conversation, how can you toss that across the table and then continue eating?"

Quinn shrugged. "I've tried ignoring it, but it isn't going away so we need to discuss it. And I'm still hungry. And this fish is delicious."

Cal leaned across the table and kept her voice low, not wanting to take the chance that there was someone in the restaurant who had brilliant hearing. "*It?* Are we talking about sex in general or you and me in particular?"

"Both." Quinn gestured to her plate and leaned across, jabbing his fork into a piece of her squid. "Your food is getting cold." He ate her squid and pointed his fork to her plate. "Damn, that's good. Do you want to swap plates?"

"No, I want you to explain your comment."

Quinn reached for his wine and wrapped his big hand around the bowl of the glass. Candlelight cast shadows across his face and turned his hair to gold, his eyes to a deeper shade of green. The skin of his throat and his forearms, exposed by his open-collar gray shirt and rolled-back sleeves, was tan. He looked fantastic and she wanted to jump him...

The urge just kept growing in intensity.

"What we did, that kiss…it's changed us," Quinn quietly said.

She couldn't argue with that. Of course it had.

"The question is, what are we going to do about it?" Quinn took a sip of his wine. "Are we going to do what we're both thinking about?"

Cal felt the need to protest, to hold her ground. "What makes you think I'm thinking about sex with you?"

"The fact that you stare at me like you want to climb all over me and do what comes naturally." Quinn looked impatient. "C'mon, Red, we've always been honest with each other, brutally so. Let's carry on doing that, okay?"

Cal wiggled in her chair, ashamed. "I know. Sorry." She bit her bottom lip and placed her fore-arms on the table. "I've always known that you were a good-looking guy. I've known that since you were thirteen and Nelly Porter grabbed you and dragged you behind the gym to kiss you senseless."

Quinn smiled. "She shoved her tongue in my mouth and I nearly had heart failure. She was my first older woman."

"She was thirteen and a half." Cal's smiled died. "But the point is that I know that women like you, that they are attracted to you, that you're hot. Intellectually, I understood it, but it never translated."

"Translated?" Quinn frowned.

Cal tapped her temple. "I got it here, but lately—" she placed a hand on her sternum and stumbled over her words "—I get it, physically." Cal dropped her head and felt the heat creep up her neck, into her cheeks. "I never expected to be attracted to you, to feel that way about you."

"I didn't either, Red, and it's growing bigger and bolder. I don't think we can carry on the way we have been living. It's driving me crazy." Quinn tugged on the open collar of his shirt. "I keep telling myself that you are my best friend and that our friendship is too important to mess up. But you have no idea how close I came to tossing you on the bed tonight when I saw you in your sexy lingerie."

Cal saw the heat in his eyes, the desire. Nothing more or less, just pure attraction untainted by manipulation or punishment. "But how could one kiss, one grope change everything?"

"Who knows?" Quinn drained his glass. "But I know that I've relived that kiss a million times, wanting and *needing* more.

"Aren't you curious?" he asked after a short silence. "If that kiss was so good, don't you wonder how good we'd be in bed?"

Cal felt hot…everywhere. The heat pooled between her legs. "I'm crazy-curious," she admitted.

"Of course, that could be because I haven't had sex since Toby," she added. Oh, how she wished she could blame her current obsession with Quinn's body—with Quinn—on the fact that she'd been in a long, dry spell.

It took a moment for those words to sink in. "You haven't had sex in five years?" he clarified.

Okay, he didn't need to look so horrified. "No. Anyway, let's change the subject."

"Let's not." Quinn lifted their joined hands and nudged her chin so she had to look at him. "Five years since you last had sex tells me that you could take or leave it. That suggests your experiences in the bedroom weren't that great. Not surprising since you were married to the biggest asshat on the west coast."

"It's not nice to speak ill of the dead," Cal told him, eyes flashing.

"I spoke ill of him when he was alive so I can when he's dead. So, am I right? Okay, I know you won't answer that, but I'll take your nonanswer as a yes." Quinn shook his head. "What an idiot."

"Can we go back to talking about risking our friendship for sex?"

"And it is a risk," Quinn said, his chest rising as he pulled in a huge breath. "I want you, but every time I think about losing you because of sex, I start backpedaling like crazy. I want a guarantee that if we sleep together, we won't let our friendship get weird."

"It's weird right now, and we haven't even slept together," Cal pointed out.

Quinn leaned back in his chair and looked stubborn. "I want the sex and I want my friend."

"There is only one thing I'm sure of when it comes to relationships, Quinn, and that's there are no guarantees. It is never how you think it's going to be."

"Is that what happened with your marriage, Cal? Did it not turn out to be as great as you expected?"

Cal forced herself to meet his eyes.

"Every time I refer to Carter or your marriage, you shut me down. You don't talk about it and you talk about everything. Especially to me. Which means that you're either still mourning him because you were crazy in love with him or you had a really bad marriage."

Cal couldn't help the shudder and she winced when Quinn's eyes sharpened. "That's it. It was bad, wasn't it?"

Oh, he saw too much, knew her too well. "Maybe I don't talk about it because I know you never liked him, because you never wanted me to marry him," Cal protested, voicing the first excuse she thought of.

"Rubbish! I never wanted you to work overseas, in dangerous countries and situations, but you did and we still talk about your work. Your marriage is over. Your husband died. Okay, so it wasn't great, but why won't you talk about it? It's not like you're the first person in the world to make a mistake."

Because she still, years later, felt like an idiot. Because she'd found herself—a strong, independent woman—in an abusive relationship and not sure how she was going to get out of it. Toby had brainwashed her into thinking she couldn't make it in the world alone. Up until the day he died and she had to make it on her own. And then she proved him wrong by surviving and then flourishing.

She'd never allow a man to do that again, to climb so far inside her head to control how she felt about herself. To control anything she did or thought. No matter how much she wanted Quinn, she'd never let him control her, dominate her. And wasn't sex a manifestation of dominance?

Or was she just projecting her memories of Toby and sex onto Quinn?

Cal tapped her finger on the stem of her wineglass, deep in thought. Quinn had never, not once, tried to control her, dominate her or manipulate her, so why did she assume he would be like that in bed? Quinn wasn't Toby...

Quinn. Was. Not. Toby. And she was not the woman she'd been with Toby. *Everything* was in her control. She could choose whether or not to have sex, how much to give or take, how much to allow. This was her life, her body.

Her heart...

She could do this.

"Talk me through it, Quinn. Sleeping with you, I mean." Her heart knew that sex with Quinn would not be like sex with Toby but her brain still needed a little convincing.

Quinn pushed his plate away and reached for the wine bottle, dumping a healthy amount in both their glasses. He smiled and it was a potent mixture of slow and sexy. "I could make it good for you, Cal... No, I would make it amazing. You need amazing. You'd leave my bed boneless, satisfied, happy. I'm a good lover."

She didn't doubt it.

"And that's not because I'm experienced but because it's important to me that my lovers enjoy it as much as I do. And you are a hundred times more important to me than anyone I've ever taken to my bed before."

Cal heard his sincerity, his growly voice sparking a firestorm over her skin.

"Sex, to me, is about so much more than my orgasm." Quinn's eyes on hers dried up all the moisture in her mouth. "It's about discovering the exact texture of your skin. Is it as creamy, everywhere, as it looks? I've always loved your freckles and I need to know if you have freckles in unusual places."

His voice was grumbly and so freakin' sexy as he continued. "I want to feel your hair tickle my stomach. I want to know whether you smell of wildflowers between your legs. I want to drown in the heat of your mouth. You have the sexiest mouth. I bet you don't know that."

He was killing her, Cal decided. Her hands and panties both felt damp with excitement. "I want to hear your moans, your breathy voice in my ear telling me what you like. I want to hold you as you shudder, feel you as you go over the edge. I want to find out what it's like making love to you, with you, Cal."

She couldn't stay here, not for one more minute. His voice had whipped her up until all she could think about was allowing him to do everything he mentioned and anything else he thought of.

"So let's find out."

Hunger, hot and hard, flared in his eyes. He stood up and reached for his wallet. "Yeah, let's."

She pushed her chair back and tossed her napkin on the table as she stood up. She looked up at him and nodded once, slowly. This was about sex, about physical relief, nothing more. She could do this...

This wasn't about control or deeper feelings or the future. Or her past. This was about walking on the wild side, tasting the storm, riding the wind. This was about Quinn.

This was about tonight. The future could look after itself.

Quinn whipped open the sliding door and placed a hand on Cal's back, urging her inside. He slammed the door shut behind him, wincing as she jumped. If she changed her mind, he'd cry like a little girl. He needed this...

He needed her.

Please don't let her change her mind.

Quinn stepped toward her, searching her face. In her eyes he saw a bit of what-the-hell-are-we-doing but nothing else that would make him back off. She wanted this, wanted him, and his heart swelled.

Quinn put his hands on her hips, swallowing a relieved sigh when her breasts flattened against his chest, when her hands slid over his pecs to his shoulders and up to his neck. He kissed her, slid his tongue into her open mouth and resisted the urge to squeeze her tighter, to suck her into him. Cal's hand dropped down his back and yanked his shirt up, trying to find the skin of his lower back. Impatient, he grabbed the back of his collar and pulled his shirt off in one vicious yank. He heard Cal suck in a hard breath and a second later her mouth was on his chest, tasting his skin above his heart with the tip of her tongue.

Such a small gesture, he thought, closing his eyes. Yet it sent a spark of pure light straight to his groin. Quinn took her face in his hands, bending his head to kiss her. He devoured her, pouring the frustration of the last few weeks of wanting her into his kiss. Cal moaned in his mouth and Quinn thought he was feeling far too much fabric and not enough skin.

He walked her backward until the back of her calves hit the sofa. "I wish I had the patience to slowly undress you, but I don't," Quinn said, his mouth against her neck. "Get naked, as quickly as possible."

Quinn yanked off his shoes as she stepped out of her heels and when his hands went to unsnap his pants, she released the ties holding up the bodice of her dress and then pushed the fabric down her hips. Her sexy dress dropped to the floor and she stood in front of him, pink lingerie and most of her endlessly creamy skin on display.

"I don't see any freckles," he murmured, his finger sliding across the tops of her round breasts.

"You're not looking closely enough," Cal replied. She nodded to his still-buttoned pants. "Need some help getting those off?"

"I can manage." Quinn smiled as he pushed his pants and boxers over his hips revealing himself to her curious gaze. Her eyes deepened to black and her body flushed.

With need. For him. Quinn felt a hundred feet tall, Hercules-strong. Unable to wait any longer, he unsnapped her bra and her breasts fell into his hands. Quinn skimmed over her breasts, across her nipples, his eyes falling to her flat stomach. He smiled when he saw her belly button ring. He dropped his hand and touched it, rolling the small diamond between his fingers.

"I remember when you got this. You were sixteen and mad at your mom because she wouldn't let you get a tattoo," he whispered.

Cal smiled. "And you bought me a chocolate milk shake and told me jokes to stop my tears." She touched his cheek and then his chin. "You hated it when I cried."

"I still hate it when you cry," Quinn told her, kissing the fingers that drifted over his lips.

Cal sucked in her bottom lip. "Please don't let this be a mistake, Quinn."

Quinn's hand lay flat across her lower stomach, warm and solid. "No matter what, Red, we'll always be friends. Nothing and nobody, not time and not this, will change that."

"Promise?"

"Promise. And I promise that I'll make this good for you."

"It's already amazing," Cal stated as his fingers slid under the lace of her panties and touched the most feminine part of her.

Man, she felt marvelous. Wet, hot, girly. God, he was rock-hard and he wanted nothing more than to slide into her, feel her engulf him, hot and ready. But this wasn't about him; this was about Cal. He'd promised to make sex wonderful for her, to allow her to feel what she never had before. He wanted to make this special, to build her up, to let her experience the magic that was fantastic sex. It felt right that he was sharing this with her, that he was showing her how hot, dirty, crazy and wonderful sex could be. They'd done so much else together, had experienced so many firsts, that it seemed, well, fitting that he should show her how amazing sex could be.

Reminding himself to go slowly, he pushed her panties down her smooth thighs and gently lowered her to the couch. He bent down, dragged his wallet out of his pants pocket and found his emergency condom. He ripped the packaging open, slid the latex on and turned to face Cal, lying on the couch, open to his gaze. With her red curls, dark blue eyes, luscious skin and that made-to-sin-with-him mouth, she was the most beautiful woman he'd seen in his life.

"God, Cal," he whispered and then moaned when

her thighs opened as he settled on top of her, his erection finding her hot, secret, girly opening.

"You haven't found any more freckles yet and you don't know if I smell like wildflowers," Cal whispered into his ear as her nails dug into the skin of his butt and she lifted her hips in that age-old invitation to come on in.

"I'll do that later," Quinn promised. He needed all of her, as much as he could get, so his tongue invaded her mouth and his cock pushed into her, finding her soft and hot and silky and perfect.

Cal wrenched her mouth away and whimpered. He stopped, looking down at her in concern. "You okay?'

A strand of red hair covered her cheek and her eyes blazed up at him. "Just don't stop. Please!"

Quinn wanted to reassure her, but he couldn't—it was all too much. He felt both honored and terrified that she needed him as much as he needed her. She was too much. So responsive, so sensitive.

Quinn pumped his hips, Cal moaned and he never wanted to stop. "Quinn! Please..."

Quinn pushed himself up on one hand and reached between them to touch her, his fingers immediately finding her special place. She bucked, moaned and her internal muscles clenched around him. She bowed her back and slammed her hips up, taking him deeper. He felt her vibrate, felt her release and, having no willpower left, let go, pulsing into her.

Quinn felt her hands running up his butt and his

back. He listened to her breathing. Instead of rolling right off as he usually he did, he took the moment to inhale her sex-and-flowers scent, enjoying the feel of her lips as she dropped tiny kisses on his jaw, her soft hands roaming his body.

When he finally lifted his head to look at her, her eyes were languid and soft and oh-so-satisfied.

"Well, that was fun. Want to do it again?" she asked with a husky laugh.

Hell yes.

Seven

Quinn looked across the picnic area at Ferguson Point in Stanley Park and noticed that Cal was surrounded by kids. She had a toddler leaning against her shoulder, another in her lap and an older girl had a slim arm around her neck. Six or seven kids, all of different ages, were sitting on the grass in front of her, fascinated by whatever she was saying.

This event—a picnic for children who'd survived a life-threatening illness—was another of the foundation's annual events. Quinn didn't mind joining her and supporting the event. He believed in what they were trying to achieve. And spending the day sitting in the sun and eating junk food in Stanley Park was good for anyone's soul, sick or not.

Kade and Brodie sat on a park bench with him, watching the activity. Some of the older kids were throwing a Frisbee. There were kids on the swings. Toddlers were chasing bubbles and squealing.

"What is she doing?" Quinn asked Brodie, gently nudging her with his elbow, wincing when he connected with little Cody's foot instead of Brodie's side. Her and Kade's brand-new son was asleep in her arms. "Sorry, sorry... Did I wake him?"

"It would take a bomb to wake Cody," Kade replied. He sat on the other side of Brodie, his arm around her shoulder. "And, from what I gathered when I walked past, Cal is telling them a story, something to do with the animals in the forest."

"She's really good with kids," Brodie said, twisting to put Cody into Kade's spare arm and snuggling into her husband's side. Cody's eyes flicked open as he was resettled, looked up at his dad and fell back asleep, utterly content.

Kade was a good dad, Quinn realized and his heart bumped. He looked across at Mac who was talking to Wren, his arm across Rosie's small chest, holding her between his legs, her back to his stomach. He was oblivious to the fact that his daughter was drooling over his hand. Kade and Mac had made the transition from bachelors to husbands to fathers easily and happily, taking the added responsibility in stride.

Quinn was proud of them for stepping up to the plate, for putting their women and their children first, for making them a priority in their lives. They'd embraced love and this new stage of their lives with enthusiasm and joy and Quinn was happy for them.

He would never make that transition, would never have to rearrange his life to make room for a family and he was okay with that. Wasn't he?

Of course you are! And really, why do you want to borrow trouble thinking like that? Don't you have enough problems dealing with your attraction to your temporary wife and best friend?

Quinn pulled his gaze off Cal to look at the panoramic view of English Bay. Yet the amazing scenery was no competition for the woman sitting on the grass, her bright hair in a long braid, freckles scattered across her nose and cheeks. God, he loved her freckles, loved that lush mouth, the fascinating dark blue of her eyes. The gorgeous dip of her back above her butt cheeks, her elegant toes, the perfection of her breasts, her pretty—

"So, is there any chance of making this fake marriage real?"

Quinn's head snapped around and he looked across the empty space where Brodie had been sitting. He'd been so focused on watching Cal he hadn't noticed Brodie leaving the bench.

His frustration with himself, and his discomfort over the fact that Cal had him under her spell, made him scowl. "What?"

"You and Cal."

"What about me and Cal?"

"You look good together, you enjoy each other's company and you're more real with her than you've ever been with any of your previous women—"

"*Real?* What does that mean?"

Kade didn't react to Quinn's hot tone; he just kept his steady gaze on Quinn's face. He tried not to squirm. "With her, you're you. The real you."

"I'm exactly the same person whomever I'm with," Quinn protested.

"You are degrees of you," Kade replied, tipping his head. "You can be charming, the life and soul of the party, a daredevil, all determination and hotheadedness. You are also a don't-give-a-toss bad boy."

Quinn thought about arguing and then realized that he couldn't think of anything to say that would counter Kade's argument.

"When you are relaxed, quieter, not trying so hard to show everyone that you're such a bad ass—that's who you are when you are with us, when you are with Cal. The real Quinn."

Right now he was the wanting-to-punch-Kade version of himself. The truth always hurts, he realized. He did use different elements of his personality to navigate different areas of his life, but that didn't mean he liked to be called on it.

"Doesn't everybody pull on different sides of their personality to get through the day? To get them through life?"

Kade nodded as his finger slid down Cody's nose,

his expression contemplative. "Sure. But it's important to have a person you can relax with, who you can drop the pretense with. Cal is your person."

No, she wasn't. Not like that. Well, maybe like that but not in a happy-ever-after way. She was his best friend and the person he was sleeping with. He was temporarily, legally bound to her and when they were done being married, they'd still be best friends.

They had to be. It was what they'd promised.

"It isn't like that," Quinn protested.

"It's like that," Kade insisted. "Why won't you see it?"

Everything was changing, Quinn thought, ignoring Kade's question. A few short months ago his life made sense. He'd been wild and free, but he was now married and sleeping with his best friend. He'd spent more time thinking about kids and families in the past weeks than he had all his life.

His world had shifted off its axis and he didn't know how to move it back, or if he even wanted to. Being a husband, having a family wasn't something he could wrap his head around, but, somewhere and somehow, he'd stopped dismissing the notion for the nonsense he'd always thought it to be.

Irritated with himself, he watched as Cal stood up. His heart stumbled as she scooped up the smallest toddler and easily settled the dark-haired boy on her hip. The child dropped his head onto her shoulder and shoved his thumb into his mouth. Cal patted heads, squeezed shoulders and started to walk toward Quinn, her cheek against that small, dark head.

God, she'd be a good mom. Even if he could imagine a life with her, he could never give her children. He'd want to give her children. Kids, for Cal, would be a deal-breaker. He knew Cal wanted a big family one day and he would never be able to give her what she truly deserved.

Sometimes he thought that he should tell her, just blurt it out and get it done. Didn't she deserve to know? He should have told her years ago, as his best friend. Then again, he hadn't told Mac or Kade. He hadn't told anyone...

Sometimes, like now, he felt like he wanted to tell Cal. That could be because he was feeling connected to her, dammit—*emotionally* connected. Great sex had the ability to create those connections and usually, when that happened, he distanced himself from the source of the connection. That couldn't happen with Cal thanks to their friendship and the wedding band on his finger.

Quinn wiped his hand across his forehead. He was being too introspective; he was overthinking and over-analyzing. *Take a step back and pull yourself together, Rayne.*

He and Cal were friends who were having sex. It wasn't something to fret over. And his secret was his to keep...

"Hi," Cal said as she approached them and patted a chubby leg. "Meet Lee, who is a cutie-pie." She flashed a smile at Kade and looked down at Cody. "God, he's gorgeous, Kade."

Kade's smile was pure pride. "Isn't he? I do really good work."

Cal grinned. "I think Brodie might have helped a bit."

Kade patted the seat beside him and stood up. "Have a seat. I'm going to put my guy in his stroller and then I might start a game of soccer." He looked in Quinn's direction. "Do you want to play?"

Quinn shook his head. "Maybe later."

Quinn watched Kade walk off and then stretched out his long legs and tipped his face to the sun. "You've had a good turnout. There are a lot of kids here."

"Yeah." Cal sat down and the little boy curled up against her chest. "My mom started this event a couple of years before she was diagnosed. She loved kids."

"As you do," Quinn said. He half turned in his seat and gripped the end of her braid between his thumb and index finger. "During your marriage, I kept expecting to hear that you were pregnant."

Distaste flashed across Cal's face and Quinn frowned, puzzled. "You didn't want kids?"

"Not then," Cal muttered. She shuddered and her arms tightened around Lee's small body. Quinn looked down and saw the child's eyes had closed. He'd stopped sucking his thumb.

Quinn ran his finger down her cheekbone, along her jaw. "I'm presuming that you'd like a family one day?"

More family talk? There was definitely something wrong with him. Quinn watched as Cal captured her bottom lip between her teeth and nodded. "Yeah, I really, really would."

He pushed the words past that expanding ball in his throat. "Then, after we're done, you're going have to marry again, find a good guy who will give you a kid or three or four."

Cal rolled her eyes. "C'mon, Quinn, since when do I need to marry to have kids? Hell, I don't even need a man to have a baby. Have you heard of sperm banks?"

Quinn looked at her horrified. "Are you insane? You can't pick the father of your children out of a database!"

"Why not?"

"Because he could be a psycho?"

"I'm sure they weed out the psychos in their screening process."

Quinn wasn't sure if she was yanking his chain or not. "No sperm banks, Cal. Seriously."

"Well, what are my other choices?" Cal demanded, leaning into his shoulder. "I suppose I could have a series of one-night stands with men I think would be good genetic material but that seems, well, tacky."

Okay, that sounded even worse than the sperm banks. The thought of another man's hands on her body made Quinn want to punch someone. "No one-night stands, Callahan."

"Well, I'm not going to fall pregnant by wind pollination, Rayne. Anyway, I'm not nearly ready to have a kid and when I am, I'll make a plan. I might even ask my best friend to donate some of his boys. He's my favorite person, is stunningly good-looking, smart as a whip and I like him. But don't tell him that."

Quinn stared at her. He blinked, trying to make sense of her words. There was no way she could possibly be asking him for the one thing he couldn't give her. No way, no how.

Life couldn't possibly be that much of a bitch.

"Take a breath before you pass out, Rayne. Jeez," Cal said, patting his thigh with his free hand. "It was just an idea that popped into my head."

"Cal—"

Cal's fingernails pushed through his jeans and dug into the skin of his thigh. "Okay, I get it, that's a solid hell no."

Hurt flashed across her face and dropped into her eyes. Her chin wobbled and Quinn felt like a toad. He pushed the words up his throat. "I'm sorry, Cal, but I could never do that."

Quinn looked at her profile and sighed. He had to tell her, had to give her the reason for his refusal. Besides, if there was anyone whom he would share this secret with, it was Cal. He might be stupidly, crazily attracted to her, but she was still his best friend. Her friendship was still more important to him than the fantastic sex. He liked and respected her. She'd trusted him to show her how amazing sex could be; he could trust her with his biggest, darkest secret.

He took a deep breath and forced the words out. "There's little I wouldn't give you, Red, but I can't give you—what did you call them?—my boys."

"I get it. You don't want to be a dad, have a family, be tied down."

Quinn pinched the bridge of his nose with his thumb and forefinger. "God, Cal, shut up a sec. Okay?"

Cal jerked her chin up, but she stopped talking and Quinn sighed. The best way to say this was just to get it out as quickly and painlessly as possible. "I can't have kids, Cal. I'm infertile."

Cal frowned. "No, you're not."

"Yeah, I am. Every couple of years the Mavericks players have a full medical, where the team docs check us out from tip to toe. The results indicated that I am infertile."

"Did they do a sperm test?"

"No, just a blood test. Apparently it's quite a rare condition, but I've got it."

"What's the condition called?"

Quinn shrugged his shoulders. "Hell if I can remember."

Cal's fist thumped his thigh. "When did you find out and why didn't you tell me?"

Quinn covered her fist with his hand. "They told me a couple of weeks before your wedding. I picked up the phone to call you, but then I remembered that you weren't talking to me." He looked at her distraught face and sighed. "Look, Cal, this isn't a big deal—not to me anyway. I've never wanted kids, never wanted the whole picket fence deal."

Cal leaned sideways and dropped a kiss on his shoulder. He felt the heat of her lips through the fabric of his hunter-green T-shirt. "I'm so sorry about that whole no-talking thing. That was my fault and it was wrong of me."

"I did call your husband a first-class moron and threatened to kidnap you to stop you from marrying him," Quinn conceded.

Cal kept her lips against his shoulder and her words whispered up to him. "Sometimes I wish you had." Before he could ask her to explain her cryptic statement, she pulled away and spoke again. "I understand why you don't want kids and marriage, Quinn."

He lifted his eyebrows. "You do?"

"It's not quantum physics. You were hurt and ignored as a child and you're scared of being hurt again. Because your parents let you down, you are reluctant to take another chance on being loved."

"Whatever," Quinn growled, hating that she was right, that she'd put his deepest fears into words and made him face them. "My not being able to have kids is not a big deal, Cal."

He wasn't sure who he was trying to convince. Himself or her?

"It is, to me," Cal stated, her tone fierce. "It's a big deal because I think you would be an amazing dad, an amazing husband. If you dropped that shield, that fear of being hurt, and allowed yourself to love, you'd be a wonderful family man."

Cal lifted her hand from his thigh and rubbed the back of her neck, her eyes on his face. "Look at you, all puzzled and weird, thinking I've lost my mind. I haven't. I just know you, Quinn, better than anybody. *I. Know. You.* You're a wonderful friend and you'd be a great husband.

"Listen," she continued, "you need to investigate this condition, find out what you can do. There are other options for you to have a family. Adoption, surrogate sperm—"

"Cal, enough!" The words shot out like bullets. He shook his head and lifted his hands. "I'm good. This is my life. I'm okay with not being able to have kids. I always have been."

Cal shook her head. "I don't buy it. You could have it all, Quinn."

Quinn shook his head and gripped her chin in his hand. "Don't you dare feel sorry for me, Red."

"This so-called infertility is just another excuse for you not to commit, not to get involved," Cal said, her expression mulish.

Okay, he wasn't going to waste his time trying to convince her. "That's your perception, Callahan. Discussion closed."

"No, it's not."

"Let's talk about Carter, your marriage and his death."

Her face closed up and her eyes turn cool. "Let's not. Ever."

"Why won't you—"

Cal stood up and the child in her arms opened his eyes and blinked at the sudden movement. "Don't do this, Quinn."

"Why are you allowed to prod and pry, but I'm not? Why don't you trust me with the truth?" Quinn demanded, following her to his feet and pushing his hands through his hair. Why did he need to know about Cal's life with Carter? The man was long dead and he didn't affect Cal's life anymore, so why did her secrets about him bother Quinn so much?

God, this was confusing and annoying. This never happened when he slept with women he didn't talk to. Quinn jammed his hands into the pockets of his jeans and rocked on his heels, frustrated. She might trust him with her body, but she didn't trust him with her past.

And that stung.

Conversations like this—hell, any conversation with Cal lately—made him feel like he was standing in a basin on six-meter swells, desperately trying to keep his balance. Too much was happening, all at the same time. He was married, living with and making love to his best friend. His marriage would end at some point in the near future and, he assumed, sex as well. Would their friendship also end?

And if it didn't, could he still be her friend without remembering the spectacular sex? Could he forget that she had three freckles on the inside of her thigh, would the memory of her breathy moans fade?

He'd said that sleeping together would cause difficulties, but he'd underestimated how many and he certainly hadn't realized the degree to which the sex would mess with his head.

Cal was now, without doubt, his biggest complication.

"Coffee."

Cal buried her head in her pillow and felt Quinn's eyes on her. She was lying on her stomach, naked, the white cotton sheet skimming the top of her butt. She felt him rolling to his side and she turned her head sideways. He was supporting himself on a bent arm and his other hand played his favorite game, joining the dots on her shoulders. He loved her freckles as much as she hated them.

"Where's my coffee?" Cal whined and he laughed.

"Good morning to you too, Red." Quinn skimmed his hand down her back and over her butt. "Did you sleep well?"

"No, because you kept waking me up," Cal muttered, squinting up at him. He had a crease in his face from the pillow, hectic stubble and bed hair and he'd never looked more beautiful.

"If I recall, you woke me up the last time." Quinn pushed a strand of hair out of her eyes and off her forehead.

She blushed and Quinn laughed. "Don't feel embarrassed, Red. Not with me."

Cal closed her eyes, turned her face back into the pillow and let out a long groan. She couldn't help it. She became an uninhibited, wild woman with him, happy to go wherever he led her. It was the only place where she allowed Quinn a measure of control over her. In every other sphere they were absolute equals.

He never questioned where she was or what she was doing and when she did explain, he listened to her activities with interest and trusted that she'd been where she said, doing what she said. He allowed her, without any fuss, to contribute to the expenses living on the boat and when she'd purchased some jewel-toned cushions to add color to the neutral palette, it had taken him three days to notice. He told her he loved whatever she was wearing but insisted he loved her birthday suit best.

He was easy to live with, but their friendship had always come easy.

Cal rolled over, pulled the sheet up to cover her breasts and pushed her hair off her face. "This is weird. Don't you think this is weird? When do you think it'll stop being weird?"

"What is weird, exactly?"

"You and I naked. Together. Friends don't get naked."

"We have, we do," Quinn replied. "Don't overthink this, Cal. We're lovers in the bedroom, friends outside of it. It doesn't have to be more complicated than that."

Cal tipped her head and seemed to consider his

words. Simple, no drama. So refreshing. She yawned and when she lifted her arm he traced the words of her white-ink tattoo across her rib cage.

"'She flies by her own wings,'" Quinn read the words aloud. "Why that phrase, Red?"

It was a statement of her independence, but, like so much else, she couldn't find the words to explain.

"When did you get the tattoo, Red?"

"About a year after Toby died."

There, she'd said his name out loud. It was, she supposed, some sort of progress.

"I like the white ink," Quinn commented. "It's feminine, pretty."

She still found it difficult to talk about her past, so she lowered her eyes and sent him a hot look, dropping her gaze to his biceps and then his chest. "You are the baddest bad boy around and, sadly, the only one without any ink. How can you still be scared of needles?" she teased.

"I'm not scared," Quinn shot back. "I just don't see the point."

Cal rolled her eyes. "I was there the night you tried to get your first tattoo, Quinn. You passed out when the guy sat down next to you and lifted the tattoo machine. Wuss. Repeat after me, I'm a scaredy-cat." Cal sang the last word in an effort to distract him.

Quinn didn't take the bait. "Why those words, Cal?"

Aargh! Stubborn man!

"I have another one."

"You're avoiding the subject and I'll let you, for now. But at some point, sometime soon, I want to know why. So... Where? I thought I'd explored every inch of your body."

Quinn pulled down the sheet and his eyes skimmed over her torso, down her belly. Her heart thumped and her skin prickled. Occasionally she forgot that he was her oldest friend. Sometimes he felt like a tantalizing mixture of new and old, of excitement and comfort.

"Where's the second tattoo?"

"Here." Cal lifted a slender foot and twisted her ankle so he could see the tiny feather on the instep of her foot. It was beautifully rendered, a subtle white and silver shot through with gentle pinks.

Quinn cupped her foot in his hand and swiped his thumb across the tattoo. "It's in memory of your mom. She always picked up feathers, wherever she went."

Cal bit her bottom lip, touched that he'd remembered. "She said they were messages from angels. I've started looking for feathers now too."

Their eyes met and, through them, their souls connected. "And do you find them?"

Cal smiled. "Yeah, I do. All the time. I choose to believe they are my mom's way of telling me she is still around, watching over me." She pulled her foot from his hand and wriggled, suddenly uncomfortable. "I suppose you think that's silly."

"Why would I?"

"Because the dead are supposed to be dead, gone."

Cal spat out the words like they were bitter on her tongue.

Quinn rolled off the bed, stood up and grabbed a pair of jeans from the back of the chair in the corner. He pulled them on, left the buttons undone and walked over to a chest of drawers, pulling out a T-shirt for Cal to wear. He handed it to her and Cal pulled it over her head, the soft blue cotton swallowing her smaller frame. She'd never quite realized how much bigger than her he was until they'd started sleeping together.

Big but gentle, in control of his strength.

Quinn lifted his shoulders to his ears before dropping them abruptly. "I think you are mentally, and spiritually, tougher than anybody I know. Anybody who lost their mother and husband within the space of two years and managed to keep going, to keep it together, has to be. And if finding feathers gives you comfort, then who am I to judge?"

Cal knew she shouldn't compare, but if this had been a conversation with Toby, then she would've been ridiculed and mocked, disparaged and called a child. God, Quinn was Toby's exact opposite.

"I'm not sure the feathers are a message from your mom, but I know how much your mom loved you, so if finding feathers makes you feel close to her, then I'm not going to judge that, Red. I have no right to."

Cal's eyes filled with tears and she felt comfortable showing him her pain. "I miss her so much, Quinn. Still."

"I know, Red. I do too."

Cal knew that to be the truth. Her mom had been his because his own mother had been so bad at the job. Rachel had celebrated his achievements with him, the sports awards, the very-impressive-but-not-brilliant report cards. She'd accompanied Cal to watch his hockey games. She'd attended his graduation. She'd been a strong and loving presence his whole life and Cal knew he flat-out missed her too.

"What do you think she'd think about this?" Quinn asked, his voice sounding strangled. "Would she approve of you and I doing this?"

Cal took a moment to respond. "I'm not sure. I mean, she loved you, but she might think it was strange, like I sometimes do. Don't you ever look at me and wonder what we are doing?'

"All the time." Quinn scratched the back of his head. "Do you want to stop?"

Hell, no! Cal dropped her head, inspected her nails and when she lifted her head again she grinned. "It's not *that* strange."

Quinn laughed and dropped a hard kiss on her mouth. "Talking about strange… My mother left a snotty voice message saying they'd expected us to visit by now, to explain why we eloped, why there wasn't a wedding, why they had to read about my marriage in the press."

Cal frowned. "You didn't tell them? Quinn! It's been nearly three months. What were you thinking?"

"I was thinking that, since I haven't spoken to my

parents or my brothers for years, I didn't need to tell them anything," Quinn replied, defensive.

"Why haven't you spoken to them?" Cal asked, swinging her legs so she sat on the edge of the bed. "Did you have another fight?"

Cal remembered their last major dustup—they'd objected to his career as a professional hockey player and he'd told them he no longer gave a damn what they thought—and after that fight, she knew his relationship with his parents and, consequently, his brothers had cooled.

"Nope. We just faded away." Quinn shrugged. "Anyway, they suggested that we have supper. To be honest, I think they want to see you, not me."

"Why? Your parents never had much time for me."

"They never had much time for anybody who didn't have an IQ of 150 or above, so don't take it personally." Quinn pushed a hand through his hair. "And I have no idea what's behind the invite. I gave up trying to figure out my family a long time ago."

"Do you want to go?"

Quinn gave her his are-you-mad look and Cal wrinkled her nose at him. "I think we should go."

Her mom was dead and her father had nearly died; family was important!

"God." He sighed and scrubbed his face with his hands. "I am quite certain I was swapped at birth. You're going to be stubborn about this, aren't you?"

"Yep."

"I'll see when we can go over," Quinn capitulated and she smiled.

Cal shook her head. "Let's not eat there. You know your mother burns water. Why don't you invite them here and I'll cook?"

"You can't cook either," Quinn pointed out. "And grilled cheese sandwiches don't count."

"Hey, I happen to be a very good cook...now."

"Then why haven't you cooked for me, *wife*?"

Cal mock-scowled at him. "Because we're frequently not home to eat. And when we are, you bring food home. Or we eat at Mac's or Kade's."

"When did you learn to cook?" he asked, obviously curious.

Cal dropped her head and her hair hid her face. Cooking had been another of Toby's efforts to turn her into the perfect wife. "Toby sent me on a couple of cooking courses." And that was all she was saying on *that* subject!

Before he could ask her to elaborate, Cal stood up and walked over to the en suite bathroom, putting a little extra sway in her hips, hoping to move him off the topic. His eyes, as she'd hoped, moved to her chest and then headed south.

"I'm going to take a shower," Cal told him. "Call your folks, your brothers, invite them to dinner. It'll be fine."

"Ack. That's too much wishful thinking for so early in the morning," Quinn grumbled.

"Right now, I'm also wishfully thinking about coffee," Cal said from the doorway of the bathroom. "Feel free to make my wishes come true."

Quinn grinned at her. "I thought I did, last night."

Yeah, he had and did. Every night.

Cal shut the bathroom door behind her, caught a glance of the happy-looking woman in the mirror and did a double take. She barely recognized her bright eyes, her naughty smile, the sheer contentment on her face. *Don't do this, Cal,* she warned herself.

Don't set yourself up for a fall.

Quinn was temporary, their marriage was temporary—it was all so very temporary. Being with Quinn, being happy like this was a wonderful treat.

But it wasn't real life and it would end.

Happiness always did.

Eight

When Quinn returned from walking his family back to the promenade, he stepped into the main salon and dropped his head to bang it against the glass door.

"I think you're right. I think you were swapped at birth," Cal said, standing next to the dining table and looking at the remains of the meal she'd spent hours preparing. The filet of beef was virtually untouched, the blueberry cheesecake was intact and there was still half a dish of rosemary-and-garlic-roasted potatoes. "Could they not have told you they are now all vegetarians? That three of them are on a raw food diet?"

Quinn stepped away from the door. "On the plus side, they did polish off the steamed vegetables."

"And a bottle of ten-year-old whiskey and three bottles of your best red wine." Cal sniffed, thoroughly annoyed.

It had been over twelve years since she'd shared any time with the Rayne family, but Cal soon remembered why she and Quinn had spent most of her childhood hanging out at her house. His relatives were, quite simply, hard work and after an interminable evening Cal understood Quinn's need to keep his distance.

Why couldn't they see the man she did? The smart, funny, successful man who would love them, spoil them, if they gave him half the chance. He didn't need to be a genius. Being Quinn—loyal, funny, responsible and mentally tough—should be enough.

"Jeez, why did they bother to come to dinner?" Cal demanded, stacking the dirty dinner plates and taking them to the kitchen. "They spent most of the time talking to each other and barely spoke to us."

Quinn picked up the dirty wineglasses and placed them on the counter next to the dishwasher. "Ah, but they did express their reservations about our marriage and Ben did tell me that I am flaunting my wealth because I'm living on a yacht."

"Ben is still the idiot I remember." Cal rolled her eyes.

Quinn did another trip to clear the dining table and after placing some serving dishes in the dishwasher, he leaned against a counter and frowned. "Jack was more reserved than normal."

Cal bit the inside of her lip and wondered whether

she should express her opinion of his brother's relationship with his long-term partner. Maybe she should just let sleeping dogs lie…

"He and Rob want to get married," Quinn told her, pouring wine into two clean glasses. Cal took the glass he held out to her and smiled her thanks. Jack and Rob marrying would be a very bad idea, especially for Jack.

"Cal? Have you got something you want to share with me?"

Dammit. The man had a master's degree in reading her body language. Cal slowly turned around, still not sure whether she had a right to say anything.

"Spit it out, Red," Quinn commanded.

She'd never told anyone about the reality of her marriage to Toby and if she didn't shut down this conversation, she'd end up telling Quinn her dirty little secret.

This wasn't a conversation she could dip her toe into and back out of when the water got a bit chilly. This was sink or swim. She didn't want to do either.

Why couldn't she keep her big mouth shut around Quinn? Surely, by now, she would've learned to? "Cal, talk to me."

"I think Jack is being abused, possibly physically, definitely verbally by Rob," Cal quietly stated.

"What?"

"You heard me," Cal replied, crossing her arms.

"Why do you think that?" Quinn asked. Cal could see he was caught between denial and disbelief. "I thought Rob was the most reasonable, rational person at the table tonight. Apart from you and me, naturally."

Cal tapped her finger against her wineglass. "He's charming, I agree, and he made an effort to talk to us, to you," Cal replied. "He was civil and we needed civil tonight to balance out the crazy."

"Then why would you think he's beating up on my brother?" Quinn asked, genuinely confused. "Either physically or verbally?"

Cal looked around the kitchen and sighed. She didn't have the energy to tidy up, but, unfortunately, the kitchen elves were on strike. And her pride wouldn't let her leave it for Quinn's cleaning lady to sort out in the morning. She put down her glass and started to rinse the dirty plates so she could place them in the dishwasher.

"I agree that nothing about Rob's behavior suggests that he's an abuser, but everything about Jack's behavior does," Cal said, keeping her voice low. God, why had she even opened up this can of rotten worms?

She was okay. She could still walk away from this subject. She *would* walk away if it got too intense. Talking about abuse made her heart race and it made her remember why she never wanted to be embroiled in a relationship again.

You're in a relationship with Quinn...

No, she wasn't, not really. They were legally married, friends outside the bedroom and lovers within it.

She'd only married Quinn to sever the last cords

tying her and Toby together. But talking about abuse felt like she was surrendering a little of the confidence she'd fought so hard to regain. She was overreacting. This was Quinn! The only person she could trust with this information. He was, first and most importantly, her friend. Her oldest, and best, *friend*.

Quinn flipped open the dishwasher and held out his hand for the wet plate. Quinn still looked expectant and Cal knew he wasn't waiting for another dish. "Jack looked at Rob every time he voiced his opinion, wanting his approval. He served Rob his food, kept asking if he needed anything. Agreed with everything he said."

"Jack's always been needy, a fusser," Quinn stated.

"This goes deeper than that. He was nervous, constantly looking for Rob's approval."

"Isn't it natural to want approval from the people we love and who love us?" Quinn asked, confused.

Cal sighed. She understood that it was difficult to accept that his tall brother was being abused by the much shorter, less bulky Rob, but she also knew that abuse had nothing to with size. Like Toby, Rob needed to have the upper hand, needed to be in control, and he knew exactly what buttons to push to get Jack to dance to his tune.

"Beneath the facade of charm, I heard Rob's patronizing condescension, the I'm-not-entirely-sure-why-I-put-up-with-him attitude. I wanted to lean across the table and smack his smarmy face," Cal said. "Trust me, Rob's a snake."

"You don't have to like him, Red, but it's a big jump from being a jerk to being an abuser."

"It's not as far as you think," Cal muttered, not entirely under her breath.

Back off, Cal. Now!

Quinn frowned at her. "Sorry, what?"

Cal shook her head and waved her words away. "Trust me on this, Quinn. Your brother is in an abusive relationship." She closed the dishwasher and, hoping to move off the subject, she nodded toward the cheesecake. "Do you want a piece?"

Quinn laid a hand on his heart and tapped his chest. "God, yes. It looks fantastic."

Cal opened the drawer to take out a knife. Cal cut two slices and placed them on a plate. He took the fork she held out and dug in.

"Poor Ben. I saw him eyeing the filet. The guy is jonesing for a steak and fries." Cal scooped up her cheesecake and slipped it into her mouth, the tart berries a perfect complement to the creamy filling and the sweet base. "Damn, that's good."

"I would never have believed that you made this if I hadn't seen you whipping it up earlier," Quinn admitted, going back for a bigger forkful.

"I'm a girl of many talents."

"You so are." Quinn looked at her and her stomach did that swirly, jumpy, bats-on-speed spin it always did when Quinn looked at her that way.

Quinn took another bite of cheesecake and frowned

at the rest of the dirty dishes. "Leave the mess. Let's take the cheesecake and wine up onto the deck."

Cal followed Quinn up the stairs as he walked toward the large, square ottomans next to the Jacuzzi. Sitting down, he patted the cushion next to him. Cal sat, tucking her feet under her bottom and resting her glass on her knee.

"Jack's an idiot if he's being abused," Quinn stated as he put the plates on the coffee table in front of them. "Seriously, one slap and he should lay charges."

He made it sound so easy, Cal thought. So black and white. He had no idea how words could be twisted and used as weapons, how cruel loved ones could really be. Abusers could win acting awards, easily able to play the victim, always stating that they couldn't understand why they were so badly treated when they loved so much. Few people understood what it felt like to live with the fear, the crazy scenarios, the accusations and the recriminations.

By the time Toby started slapping her, her confidence had been smashed to smithereens. Regaining her sense of worth and finding herself again had been a battle of epic proportions.

"I just don't understand how someone can put up with that crap," Quinn said, leaning back and lifting a forkful of cheesecake to his mouth. "It doesn't make sense to me."

It never made sense to anyone until they were walking through the sludge of an abusive relationship, not

sure how they got into this swamp and having no way
to get out. And to Quinn, who was so self-reliant and
confident in who and what he was, it was an anathema.

Quinn waved his fork in her direction. "So, tell me
why you think Rob is abusing Jack."

Cal looked into her wineglass, thinking furiously.
This was a watershed moment and she had to decide
whether to own it. She either had to tell Quinn about
her rotten marriage and her abusive husband or she had
to shove it back in the corner and pretend it had never
happened. She either had to trust him with all of the
truth or nothing at all.

Quinn would…what? Hit her? Disparage her? Mock
her? Of course he wouldn't. Quinn wasn't that type of
man. Hadn't she told him that she knew him? And she
did. Quinn wouldn't lose his temper. He'd control his
reaction and she'd be safe.

Of course he would—this was *Quinn*.

Besides, telling Quinn wasn't about how he'd react
but about whether she had the strength to do this, the
courage to face her past. She'd grown so much in the
past five years and she was a new Cal, a better version
of the girl she'd been before she'd met Toby.

Telling somebody, telling Quinn, meant freedom.
She would be shining a light on her dark past.

Releasing her pain would heal her. It would give
her closure.

Didn't she deserve that? Cal finally acknowledged
that maybe she did.

Her decision made, Cal lifted her eyes. "Before I go into that, I need to tell you something…and it's linked, in a roundabout way, to your question about Jack."

Quinn looked puzzled. "Okay."

"I asked you to marry me for a reason."

Quinn frowned, confused. "Yeah, I needed to look better in the press and you needed some distance from the social swirl."

Cal shook her head. "All true, but there was another reason, one I haven't told you."

"Okay, that sounds ominous. What?"

Cal explained about the inheritance, told him how she needed to be free of Toby. "I don't need his money. My mom left me a trust fund and I stand to inherit a bundle from my dad."

Quinn looked astounded. "You walked away from $200 million?"

"I couldn't take his money. It was…" Cal hesitated. "It was tainted. I'll explain why, but let me go back to my comment about Rob's abuse of Jack." Cal sucked in a deep breath, looking for her courage. "The thing is, Quinn, I can recognize controlling behavior from a hundred yards away. I was married to a man who controlled everything I did, everything I said."

Quinn cocked his head. It would take a moment for the truth to sink in—it always did.

"I was Toby's possession, just like Jack is Rob's," Cal continued.

Cal watched as his protective instincts kicked in and

anger jumped into his eyes. "Go on," he said, his jaw tight.

"In hindsight, there were subtle hints of his controlling streak when we were engaged, but I thought he was just trying to protect me. After we married it got progressively worse."

Quinn bounded to his feet and loomed over her, his hands on his hips and his face suffused with anger. Cal felt a touch of panic, but she pushed the feeling away and pulled in a deep breath. This was Quinn. Quinn would *never* hurt her.

"Why the hell did you stay with him? Why didn't you divorce him? Why didn't you walk?"

He made it sound so simple; yet, at the time, it hadn't been.

Quinn looked down at her, now bewildered as well as furious. "Why didn't you call me? Jesus, Cal, why the hell didn't you tell me about this? I would've—"

"You would've punched him and caused a scene," Cal told him, her voice firm. "Then he would've pressed charges and you'd have ended up in jail, convicted for aggravated assault. I couldn't do that. I couldn't allow you to destroy your career."

"My career isn't that fragile."

Toby had ruined so much that she hadn't been prepared to take the chance.

Quinn pushed his fingertips into his forehead, upset and angry about something that had happened years ago. Cal reminded herself that he wasn't angry with her but at what had happened to her. He had such a good heart and he was incredibly protective of the people he allowed into his life. She loved that about him. She loved him...

Cal felt fear roll over her, hot and terrifying. She couldn't love Quinn—that wasn't part of the deal. Anything other than being part time lovers and full time friends wasn't part of the plan. She couldn't love Quinn. It wasn't safe to love Quinn.

She couldn't think of that now. Maybe she wouldn't think about it again at all.

She had to tell him the rest of her story or she never would.

"He was also physically abusive."

It would take a moment for the truth to sink in.

"What did you say?"

"Toby liked to use force to get his point across."

"Carter hurt you?" Quinn's roar was louder this time and Cal winced. Oh, God, he was losing it. Anger, dark and dangerous, sparked in his eyes and every single muscle in his body was taut. She had to bring him down; she had to diffuse the situation.

"It wasn't that bad, Quinn." Cal placed a hand on his arm. "He slapped me a couple of times. It was mainly verbal—"

"Don't you dare defend him!" Quinn linked his hands behind his head, incandescently angry. "He raised his hand to you—there is no excuse!"

It was important for her to keep calm. Arguing with him wouldn't help.

"I'm not defending him, Quinn, I'm trying to explain what happened."

"When did he start hitting you?" Quinn demanded, the cords in his neck tight.

Dammit, he would have to ask that question. "About six months after we married," Cal admitted.

"And you stayed with him for another year?" Quinn shouted. "I don't understand this, you! Why didn't you bail?"

"Because, by then, I had no self-confidence. He told me he would destroy me and my father if I walked out on him."

"And you believed him? Come on, Red, you are smarter than that!"

Cal wrapped her arms around her bent knees and tried not to feel hurt. Quinn didn't understand. "I used to judge women who stayed in abusive relationships too. It's easy to stand on that pedestal, but Toby knocked me off it with a single slap."

Her gentle rebuke hit its mark. The fire went out of Quinn's eyes, but the tension in his body remained. He pulled in a deep breath and then expelled the air and rolled his head. After a few minutes he walked back to the daybed and sat down next to her.

Quinn picked up her hand and threaded his fingers between hers. The anger was still there, but it was under control. "So, explain it to me. Why did you stay with him, Cal? I can't understand why you didn't leave the first time he hurt you. You know, you *knew*, better than that."

Shame and embarrassment rolled through her. "I told myself I didn't want my big, fancy, expensive wedding to be a waste of money—a stupid reason—and I didn't want to admit that I'd made a huge mistake. Pride and stubbornness played a part."

"Oh, Cal."

"Mostly, I didn't want to look like a fool," Cal admitted and wrinkled her nose.

"Did you ever think about leaving him?"

"I was leaving him," Cal said. "The day before the accident I told him that I was filing for divorce. We had a huge fight and he told me he would destroy me. Destroy my father. Then he punched me, really hard, in the ribs."

She saw anger roll through him again, hot and powerful. "God, I so want to find Carter's grave, dig him up and beat him back to death."

"He broke three ribs. After his death, the press reports said that I was too shocked to cry, that I was beyond tears. All I could think about was that he couldn't hurt me again. I wouldn't have to deal with a messy divorce, with the drama that would follow. I felt like I'd received a get-out-of-jail-free card." Cal looked at him with wide eyes. "Is that wrong?"

Quinn shrugged. "Not from where I'm sitting." He

squeezed her hand. "You could've called me, Cal. I would've helped."

"I know, but I felt..."

"Like a fool?"

"Yeah. I thought that since I'd gotten myself into the situation I needed to get myself out." Cal pulled their joined hands into her lap and leaned against his shoulder. "I was very young and very dumb. I was grieving my mom's death and he made me feel bright and beautiful and, I guess, safe. Protected."

"I was also there. Didn't I make you feel like that?" Quinn demanded,

Cal shook her head. "Toby spoiled me. You've never done that. You treat me like an equal, like an adult. Toby promised that my life would be drama-free with him. After Mom died, I wanted that."

"Life is never drama-free."

"I know that now," Cal said. "I'm sorry I didn't tell you, didn't ask for your help, that I haven't told you about this before. It was my ugly little secret."

"We all have secrets, Cal, but nothing about you— not even your secrets—can ever be ugly." Quinn turned toward her and placed his hand on her cheek. The tenderness and regret in his eyes made her heart trip. "I wish you'd come to me."

Cal tasted tears in the back of her throat. "I do too. I know now you would've been there for me, Quinn, just like I know that you would be there for Jack if he allowed you to be." Cal mimicked Quinn's action and put her hand on his rough, stubbled jaw. "You're such a good man, Q, even if you don't believe it half the time."

"Not so good," Quinn said, his voice rough with emotion.

Cal shook her head. "You'll never convince me of that. You are both tender and strong and that combination floors me."

Tenderness flared in Quinn's light eyes, along with desire and protectiveness.

She couldn't resist him.

Nine

"Red—God, why can't I resist you?"

His eyes roamed over her face, looking at her like he was seeing her for the first time. And Cal knew that, even if it was just temporary, their friendship had retreated to make room for a blazing love affair.

It might only last the night or it might be strong enough to withstand the passage of time. No matter how long it lasted, she would enjoy him, as much as she could.

"I need you. I need to love you right here, right now, in the dark, in the cold night air," Quinn told her, his hands reaching for the belt that held her rich purple wraparound jersey together. His hands pulled the fabric apart and he skimmed her torso, cupped her breasts while his tongue invaded her mouth, sliding against hers in a dance that was as exciting as it had been the first time he kissed her on the terrace at the masked ball.

"You taste so good." He broke the contact with her mouth to murmur the words.

Cal moaned and her hands slid over his chest, down his waist to grip his hips. He hadn't bothered with a coat so she had easy access to the buttons on his shirt and she went to work on them. She soon felt the contrast of the chilly night air and his superhot skin. Cal felt his hand under the cup of her bra and she shivered, excitement skittering over her. These were hands that knew her, knew what she liked, knew how to touch her.

Quinn pushed Cal's shirt down and off her arms and he groaned when he pulled his head back to look at her lacy bra barely covering her creamy breasts. He dropped his head to pull her nipple into his mouth, tasting her through the barrier of the lace. Cal linked both arms around his head and held him to her. She needed this, needed him to need her, to crave her. She felt powerful and feminine, confident and sexy. Strong.

God, she felt strong.

Quinn's hands dropped to her stomach, fumbling as he tried to open the buttons on her jeans. He cursed, sounding uncharacteristically impatient. "I need you. I need to be inside you, loving you."

Quinn groaned, his mouth on hers as he pushed her jeans and thong down her legs. She kicked the garments off and moaned when his fingers stroked her with exquisite care. "So hot, so warm. Mine."

God, she was. *His, only his.*

Cal snapped open the button to his jeans, tugged down his fly and Quinn sighed when her hand found him, long, strong and so hard. She couldn't wait, couldn't cope with his drive-her-crazy foreplay tonight. She just wanted him inside her. Completing her.

Quinn shucked his clothes and pushed her down onto the ottoman. With his hands on her thighs, he gently pushed her legs apart. He leaned over her, his expression hot and hard and intense and, with a lot of passion and little finesse, he entered her with one long, fluid, desperate stroke. She was wet and ready for him. He stopped for a moment, his arms straight out as he hovered above her, her astonishment at how in sync they were reflected in his eyes. He was rock-hard and ready and she was very, very willing.

She could feel every luscious inch of him, skin on skin, her wet warmth coating him, his head nudging her womb. He felt amazing and... *God!*

"Quinn!" Cal smacked his shoulder with her fist and he pulled his head back to look down into her face.

"What? What's wrong?" he demanded, his voice hoarse with need.

"Condom! You're not wearing one."

Quinn pushed himself up on his hands to hover over her. She really didn't want him to pull out. She loved the intimacy of making love to him without a barrier. It felt real…

"I'm clean and I'm—" he choked on the words "—you know…a genetic dead end." He supported himself on one hand and she saw the muscles in his shoulders and biceps bunch as he lifted his thumb to caress her cheekbone. "If I have to run downstairs for a condom, I will, crying all the way. But I've always used a condom and I was tested last month. I'm clean, there's no chance of you falling pregnant and I just want to make love to you, feel every inch of you, with no barriers between us. Because, God, you feel amazing."

She clenched her internal muscles, involuntarily responding to the emotional plea beneath his words. His jaw was rigid and she could see he was using every speck of willpower he had to stop himself from plunging into her.

"Okay, yes," Cal said and her hands flew over his ribs, down his hips and over his butt, pulling him deeper into her. "Move, Quinn, I need you."

"Not as much as I need you, baby," Quinn growled as he forced himself to keep the pace slow. Cal whimpered with need, slammed her hips up, driving him deeper inside.

"Harder, deeper, faster," Cal chanted.

Quinn had no problem obeying that particular order and he pistoned into her, his hand under her hips to tilt her pelvis up so she could take him deeper. She suspected he was a knife's edge away from losing it and she wanted him sharing this with her.

Cal lifted her hands between their bodies to hold his face. She stared into his eyes, blue clashing with green, and smiled. "Let's fly together, Quinn."

Quinn nodded. "Now?"

"Now."

Cal let herself dissolve around Quinn, her body shaking with her intense orgasm. Love, hot and powerful, roared through her as Quinn groaned and threw his head back. She felt him come deep inside her.

His, Cal decided. Only his.

Cal rolled over and, not finding Quinn, put her hand out to pat his side of the bed. Frowning, she opened her eyes. Hearing the sound of water running, she looked at the closed bathroom door. Cal sat up, grateful for a moment alone, a little time to think.

Last night she suspected that she might be in love with Quinn. In the cold light of morning she knew it to be true. She'd fallen head over heels in love with her oldest friend.

Idiot.

Had she really been stupid enough to think he was a safe bet, to think she'd be immune to his charm, his quirky sense of humor, to that luscious body and to-hell-with-you attitude? He was the least safe person in the world to love. Yet here she was, feeling all those crazy emotions she'd swore she'd never feel again. She wasn't supposed to be thinking of him in terms of commit-ment and forever. Quinn didn't do commitment and he had no concept of forever. He married her because he needed an out, a way to mend some fences. He married her because he trusted her to not make waves, to not make demands on him that he wouldn't be able to meet.

Quinn wasn't perfect, but she didn't need him to be. He was perfect for her. He was strong enough to allow her to be strong. They argued, but he didn't overpower her. He didn't force his opinion on her. He trusted her to be the best version of herself, was strong enough to deal with the broken bits of her, adult enough to know that everyone had their quirks.

He knew her, flaws and all. Better than that, he ac-cepted her, flaws and all.

For that reason, and a million others, she loved him. In a soul-mates, be-mine-forever way.

The way he'd made love to her last night, both on the deck and later in this bed—the way he'd held her like she was precious and perfect—gave her hope. She felt excitement bubble and pop in her stomach. Maybe they had a shot...

"You're looking a bit dopey, Red."

Cal jerked her head up. Quinn's shoulder pressed into the door frame and a white towel around his hips was a perfect contrast to his tanned skin. He looked as gorgeous as ever—and as remote as the International Space Station. Unlike her, Quinn wasn't having a warm and fuzzy, I-love-you moment.

"Hi."

Quinn lifted an inquiring eyebrow. "What's up?" he asked, stalking into the room. "You have your thinking face on."

Damn, he knew her so well.

"You might as well spit it out, Red. You know you want to."

She did. She wanted to tell him how she felt, wanted to admit to him—and to herself—that she wanted a real marriage between them, something that would see them through to the end of their lives. She wanted to be the brave, strong, confident woman she'd worked hard to be and ask him if he felt the same, ask him whether he could love her like she needed to be loved.

Cal wrapped her arms around her knees, biting down on her bottom lip. "I could tell you, but I don't know if you want to hear what I have to say."

Quinn's eyes hardened and turned bleak. "Are you going to tell me something else about Carter that I won't like?"

"No. I told you about the abuse and the inheritance and that's it," Cal replied.

"Then what is it?" Quinn asked, looking at his watch. "And, sorry, I don't mean to rush you, but I need to get to headquarters for a strategy meeting with Mac and Kade."

She couldn't just blurt this out on the fly. They needed time to talk about it. Cal blew air into her cheeks. "Leave it. We can talk later."

Quinn gripped the bridge of his nose, obviously frustrated. "Cal, just say it."

Well, okay then. Cal kept her eyes on his as she spoke her truth, her voice shaking. "I'm in love with you and I want to spend the rest of my life with you. I want this marriage. I want you."

Happiness flared in his eyes but quickly died as confusion and fear stomped over that fragile emotion. Quinn rubbed his hand over his jaw and then moved it to rub the back of his neck. "God, Cal. That was not what I expected to hear."

"Yeah, I figured."

"I'm not sure what you want me to say…"

Cal pushed her curls off her face. "It's not about what I *want* you to say, Quinn. I'd just like to know if you think it's a possibility…whether you might, someday, feel the same."

Quinn disappeared into his walk-in closet and when he reappeared five minutes later, he was dressed in track pants and a Mavericks hoodie. He carried his shoes to the bed, sat down on the edge and slowly pulled on his socks.

Cal waited for him to speak and when he did, his words were precise and deliberate. "I think this is all going a bit fast. Last night was emotional and I realize that talking about Carter was difficult for you. The floodgates opened and you released a lot of feelings and I think you might be confusing that release with love. Could that be possible?"

Cal considered his words. Nope, she decided. She was definitely in love with him. "Sorry, that's not it."

Quinn bent over and stared at his sneakers before tying the laces. "The sex between us is amazing, Red, and we're good friends. That doesn't mean we are in love." Quinn sat up and looked at her, his expression determined. "*If* this is happening, then we need to take a step back, figure out what the hell we're doing before we make plans and promises that will blow up in our faces."

Cal nodded, conscious of the slow bruise forming on her heart. "You still haven't told me if you love me or not."

Quinn stood up and slapped his hands on his hips. He didn't speak and when Cal finally looked up, she saw fear and confusion in his eyes. "I don't know, Cal. I don't know what I feel. This—*you*—it's all a bit too much." He glanced at his watch and grimaced. "Let's think about this, step away from the emotion and consider what we're doing. What we're risking."

Cal clearly heard what he wanted to say but couldn't because he didn't want to hurt her: *What you're doing, what you're risking.*

He was giving her an out, a way to go back to sex without the messy complication of love.

Quinn picked up his wallet and cell phone and jammed them into the pockets of his hoodie. "I have a…thing…this evening. You?"

Cal lifted her chin, knowing damn well he didn't

have plans since they'd discussed seeing a movie to-night. But her pride wouldn't let him see her disappoint-ment, wouldn't permit her to ask for anything more. "I have a *thing* too."

Quinn nodded and walked to the side of the bed. Cal kept her face tipped, waiting for his customary see-you-later, open-mouth kiss, but he kissed the top of her head instead.

It was the age-old, you're-looking-for-more-than-I-can-give-you brush-off.

Message received, Quinn. Message received.

A week passed and Cal wasn't sure why she was at the Mavericks arena midmorning, especially since she had work piling up on her desk back at the foundation. If pressed, she supposed she could say she'd come to talk to Quinn about their upcoming schedules, whether he could attend a theater production with her later in the month. There were a dozen questions she could ask, but nothing that couldn't be resolved during a two-minute phone call or later that day when they touched base back at home…

Home. It might be a good idea if she stopped think-ing of the yacht in those terms.

Coming to the arena had been an impulsive decision but one that was rooted in her need to see Quinn. She wanted to talk him into having lunch with her, to try and push past the barrier her impulsive declaration of love had created between them a week ago. They were still living together, still sleeping in the same bed, still making love. But they weren't communicating. They were two people who were sharing his space and their bodies and nothing else. She didn't think she could live like this for much longer. She was back in purgatory, except this time they were lovers but not friends. She felt angry and sad and, yes, disappointed.

They were acting exactly how they'd said they never would and they were hurting each other. They needed to break this impasse. One of them had to be brave enough to walk away before they destroyed their friendship. She'd raised the subject of love; she'd changed the parameters of their marriage by uttering the *L* word so it was her responsibility to fix what was broken.

While she waited for Quinn to call an end to the practice session, she thought how much she loved to watch him skate. Cal propped her feet up onto the boards that lined the rink. He was poetry in motion, at home on the ice just as he was on land. Dressed in jeans and a long-sleeved T-shirt with a sleeveless jacket over his broad chest, he looked bold and determined.

And utterly in charge.

His players took his direction easily and quickly and, while they respected him, they certainly weren't scared of him. It was obvious they gave him a thousand percent all the time. You didn't work that hard for someone unless you were inspired to do so.

He pulled no punches. No one was spared his praise or his sharp tongue. Even Mac, his partner, was treated exactly the same as the rest of the players. On the ice there was only one boss and Quinn was it. That amount of intensity, that power was…well, it made her panties heat up.

Cal, digging into a bag of chips, looked up when she heard the click-clack of heels. She smiled at Wren, who was making her way to her seat in the first row back from the rink. On the ice, Quinn was barking orders to his squad, short blond hair glinting in the overhead lights.

"I heard you were here," Wren said, bending down to kiss her cheek before dunking her hand in the bag of chips.

"Sneaky thief," Cal muttered as Wren settled into the chair next to her.

"You can't eat a mega-sized bag of chips by yourself. You'll get fat," Wren told her. "I'm just being a good friend, helping you out."

"Yeah, yeah," Cal replied and placed the bag between them. She nodded to the thick envelope on Wren's knees. "And that?"

Wren patted the envelope and popped another chip in her mouth. After swallowing, she passed the envelope to Cal and smiled. "That, my darling, is the measure of our success. You actually did it."

"Did what?" Cal asked, opening the envelope and pulling out a sheaf of papers.

"The rehabilitation of Rayne. Those are the photocopies of every article mentioning you or Quinn over the past month and every single one is positive. Quinn is redeemed. By the love of a good woman."

Cal started flipping through the papers, stopping now and again to read a headline, to look at a photograph. There was one of them kissing outside the coffee shop close to her office, another of them in Stanley Park at the picnic, walking hand in hand and laughing. Old Friends, New Lovers read one headline. Are Quinn and Cal Vancouver's Most Romantic Couple? Is It True Love?

"The Mavericks brand is stronger than ever and trust in Quinn, as a person and as a coach, has been restored. Instead of baying for his blood, the press is now baying for babies." Wren's hand dipped into the bag again and she stood. "I'll leave you to take a look through those. Thanks, Cal. I could never have whipped him into shape on my own."

Baying for babies? Cal felt her heart tighten. That was never going to happen and it made her feel sad, a little sick.

If Quinn wanted a family or marriage, if he wanted *her*, he would've initiated a discussion about their future. He would've asked to talk about her ill-timed and unwelcome declaration seven days ago.

His silence on the subject said everything she needed to hear: he absolutely wasn't interested in anything more than what they had.

He'd married her for a reason and since that goal had been achieved, there was no rationale for staying married. It was time to cut her losses and try to move on.

Cal tipped her head to look up into Wren's lovely face. "Does this mean we can start, uh, dialing it down?"

"Sorry?" Wren asked, confused.

Cal shoved her fingers into her hair, lifting and pushing the curls back. "That was the plan—we make it look good and then we start drifting apart."

Wren waved at the papers in Cal's lap. "If you faked everything, then I commend you on your magnificent acting." Wren placed her hands on her hips and scowled. "But I've been doing this for a long time and I know fake when I see it. This isn't one of those times."

"We're friends."

"Pffft. You are so much more than that. You are good together. Damn, girl, you are the best thing that's happened to that man in a very long time. You don't seem unhappy either, so why on earth do you want it to end?"

She didn't, but what she wanted was beside the point. "It will end, Wren."

"Then you are both idiots," Wren told her before bending down and kissing Cal's cheek. "I hope you both change your minds because yours could be an amazing love story."

Wren touched Cal's shoulder and gave her a sad smile before walking away. Cal gathered the articles together and pushed the papers back into the envelope and laid it face down on her lap.

She had to start controlling her attraction to Quinn instead of letting attraction control her. If she didn't, she would find herself in the same situation she'd been in years ago, hopelessly in love with a man who didn't love her, without any emotional protection or power.

Oh, wait…that horse had already bolted from the stable; she already loved Quinn. She loved him like a friend; she loved him as a lover. She simply, deeply, profoundly loved him, in every way a woman could.

Okay… She loved him, but that didn't mean she couldn't protect herself. She was not prepared to let all rational thought disappear and capriciousness rule. She'd learned her lesson well.

Unlike her younger self, she could now look at relationships, and men, and see them clearly. Quinn didn't love her, not romantically in a I-want-to-spend-the-next-sixty-years-with-you type of way. He loved making love to her. Maybe because she was handy and she was the only person he could—without making waves and headlines—have sex with. Quinn was also exceptionally good at separating his emotions from, well, anything and she knew he could easily separate their friendship from making love.

She didn't have any desire to change Quinn. Yeah, her goal had been to rehabilitate his reputation, but she had no desire to rehabilitate him. She'd always loved him for who he was, the adrenaline junkie who'd jump off buildings with a parachute strapped to his back, who laughed like a maniac on roller-coaster rides, who leaped from one crazy stunt to another in order to feel alive. Because he'd spent his childhood hoping to be noticed, and she understood his need to feel alive, to feel free. She understood what motivated his crazy...

She loved him. She understood him. She would feel like she'd had her limb amputated when they parted, but they had to end this. Her heart was already battered and bruised, but that was better than having her psyche and her soul decimated.

She and Quinn needed to have a serious talk about splitting up. They needed to come up with a plan for how to navigate the next couple of months. They had to start winding down their relationship, start spending some public and private time apart. They had to be strategic in how they drifted away from each other.

She didn't want the public to blame Quinn. She didn't want to reverse the current wave of good press he was receiving. Her father wanted to return to work and so could she; there were problems with the projects in Botswana, India and Belize she needed to attend to. They could blame her work, distance and time apart for the breakup of their marriage. Everyone understood that long-distance relationships never worked...

Cal pulled a bottle of water from her bag and twisted the cap. She took a long swallow and replaced the cap as Quinn called a break.

Quinn's eyes met hers across the ice and he lifted a finger to tell her he'd be with her shortly. Happy to wait, Cal watched as the players glided across the ice, most of them in her direction. As they removed their helmets, she recognized some faces from the barbecue on Quinn's yacht last weekend.

"Hey, Cal."

Cal dropped her feet and leaned forward, smiling. "Hey Matt, Jude. Beckett."

Beckett sent her a bold smile. "*Mrs*. Boss Lady."

Cal leaned back and crossed her legs, amused when six eyes followed the very prosaic movement of her denim-covered legs tucked into knee-high leather boots. God, they looked so young, so fresh-faced. Compared to Quinn, they looked like boys. These boys still had a lot of living to do. They needed to experience a little trouble, needed to have their hearts broken and learn a couple of life lessons. Then their pretty-boy faces would become truly attractive.

Cal jerked her attention from her thoughts to their conversation.

"So, what are we doing tonight?" Beckett demanded, sliding guards onto the blades of his skates before swinging open the door that would take him off the ice. He walked between Cal and the boards and dropped into the chair next to her, sending her an easy, confident grin. "FOMO's, Up Close or Bottoms Up?"

"What's FOMO's?" Cal asked, interested. She knew that Up Close was a club and that Bottoms Up was a sports bar owned by Kade, Mac and Quinn.

Beckett stretched out his arms and his hand brushed Cal's shoulder as he rested it against the back of her chair. Not wanting to give him any ideas—he was far too slick for his age—Cal leaned forward and rested her elbows on her knees.

"It's a place downtown," Beckett replied. "Want to come?"

Matt flicked a glance toward Quinn and shook his head. "Uh, Beck, not a great idea. Boss man wouldn't like it."

Cal frowned. The comment sliced a bit too close to the bone. "Last time I checked, I was a grown-up and I make my own decisions. Quinn doesn't do that for me."

Jude pinched the bridge of his nose. "Seriously, Cal, he really won't like you…"

Beckett's laugh was rich. "If she wants to come, let her. We'll be there from around ten."

Who went out at ten? Ten was when most people were thinking about bed, or sitting in their pj's eating ice cream. "Ten?"

Beckett picked up the end of her braid and rolled it in his fingers. "Maybe you are too old to party with us." Cal almost didn't notice the sly look he sent Quinn, the smirk to his fallen-angel mouth. "Maybe you should just be a good wife and stay in. Quinn *definitely* won't like it."

She knew she was being played, but she couldn't bear the thought of this young whippersnapper thinking anyone had control over her.

Cal jerked her braid out of his fingers. "For your information, Quinn has no say about what I do or who I do it with."

Beckett lifted an amused eyebrow. "Okay then, *Mrs. Rayne*. FOMO's, at ten. Do you want us to collect you?"

"I think I can get there under my own steam," Cal told him, her tone slightly acidic.

"Get where?"

She hadn't heard Quinn's silent approach, but Matt and Jude's tense body language should've given her a hint. Beckett's sly smirk deepened and Quinn's fierce frown didn't intimidate him in the least. "Hey, boss. Just to let you know, Callahan is joining us at FOMO's tonight, if you want to hang out."

Quinn's eyebrows nearly disappeared into his hairline. "At FOMO's?" He folded his arms across his chest and scowled. "No, she's not."

Beckett stood up and shrugged. "I told her you wouldn't like it, but she said you're not the boss of her."

"Hey, I'm right here!" Cal stated.

"You are *not* going to FOMO's."

Cal tilted her head. Right, this was just one small reminder as to why she shouldn't want to stay married. Nobody was allowed to make decisions about any aspect of her life but her. "I am. And you are not going to stop me."

Cal stood up as Beckett, Jude and Matt made a tactical retreat.

Quinn looked like he was making an effort to hold on to his temper. "Cal, listen to me. FOMO's—"

"You can't tell me what to do, Rayne! We're sleeping together and that's it." Cal pulled her bag over her shoulder. "You are never going to control me, tell me what to do or how to do it. I will never allow a man that measure of control again."

"I'm not trying to control you! I'm trying to tell you that FOMO's is—"

"Save it! I'm not going to listen!" Cal wasn't interested in anything more he had to say, her temper now on a low simmer. What was it about men and their need to control the situation, control how their women acted? Was it ego? Stupidity? A rush of blood to the head? Whatever it was, she wasn't going to play his game. She might like his bossy ways in the bedroom, but everything else—her money, her clothes, what she did and how she did it—was strictly off-limits.

She loved him and he didn't love her. It was that simple. But even if he did fall to the floor and beg her to spend the next sixty years with him, she would never grant him the right to dictate her actions.

"I'm done with this conversation," Cal told him, her voice quiet and cold. She picked up the envelope and slapped it against his chest. "Wren dropped these off. When you see them, maybe you'll agree that we need to talk. We need to start thinking about dialing this down."

"What are you talking about?" Quinn raised his voice as she started to walk up the stairs to the exit. "Come back here, I need you to understand why I won't allow you to go to FOMO's."

Cal half turned and raised one shoulder, her face flushed with anger. Did he really use the word *allow*? After everything she'd told him? Seriously? "*Allow?* You won't allow me to go? Who the hell do you think you are? I don't answer to you, Rayne. I am not one of your players or one of your bimbo girlfriends who will roll over at your command!"

"Callahan!" Quinn growled.

Cal just kept on walking.

Yeah, they really needed to put some distance between them.

Ten

Black and pink and purple, Cal thought as she walked into FOMO's. Lots of black and pink and purple. Not her favorite color combination. Cal slid into a small space near two guys standing at the bar. Between attempts to catch the eye of a bartender, she looked around for Beckett or any of the Mavericks players. She couldn't see them and she wondered, not for the first time, what she was doing here.

Clubs weren't her scene; the repetitive thumping of the music gave her an earache and the flashing neon lasers gave her a headache. The smell of liquor and cologne and perfume clogged her nose and she felt claustrophobic from the bodies pressing her against the bar.

"What can I get you?" the barman shouted at her,

his white teeth flashing and his dreadlocks bobbing in time to the beat.

A taxi? An oxygen mask? "A club soda and lime. Hey, have you seen the Mavericks players in here tonight?"

His hands deftly assembled her drink, but his eyes gave her an up-and-down look. "Honey, you're a little old and a lot overdressed to catch their eye."

"Thanks," Cal said, her tone dry. "Have you seen them?"

He nodded toward a floating staircase in the corner. "They are upstairs." He slid the glass toward her. "You look really familiar. Do I know you?"

"No," Cal quickly answered, but she didn't kid herself that she wouldn't be recognized sometime soon. Not everyone in the club was drunk or stoned and she could guarantee that the vast majority of those who were still sober were Mavericks fans.

"I have that type of face," Cal told him. She reached into the pocket of her tight skinny jeans and pulled out a bill. Before she could hand it over, she felt a hard body press her into the bar and a hand shot past her face, strong fingers holding a twenty-dollar bill.

Cal sighed when the bartender took the man's money and not hers. She frowned, waving her money at him. "I want to pay for my own drink. No offense intended."

"I've been offended all damn day," the familiar voice growled in her ear. "I was offended when you flounced away, when you wouldn't answer any of the ten calls I made to you, when you didn't come home before coming here."

Dammit. Quinn had tracked her down and he was here, stalking her. Not that his presence was too much of a surprise. Quinn wasn't one to walk away from a fight.

"Quinn and his missus!" The bartender held up his knuckles for Quinn to bump. "Haven't seen you in here for ages, man!"

"Yeah, wives tend to frown on their husbands visiting FOMO's, Galen."

"That's the truth, dude."

He knew the bartender, which meant he was very familiar with this club. Cal looked at the raised dance floor to the right of the bar and sighed at the skimpily clad women—girls—writhing and grinding. It was probably one of his favorite hunting grounds.

"What are you doing here, man? And why did you bring your woman?"

"Cal and I were on our way to dinner and I wanted to stop in and check on my boys. They behaving themselves?" Quinn asked.

Galen nodded to the floating staircase. "They're upstairs, blowing off some steam. No paparazzi up there, no dealers, just some of their regular girls."

Quinn nodded. "Let me know if that changes."

"Will do, boss man."

Galen passed Quinn a beer and he wrapped his fingers around the neck of the bottle and the other hand around her wrist. She tugged at his hold and he bent his head toward hers. She was sure that anyone watching him would think he was whispering something sexy in her ear, but his words were anything but. "You. Stay."

"I am not a dog! You don't get to tell me to sit and stay!" Cal shot back, wondering how she could be so annoyed with someone who smelled so good and turned her insides to mush.

"Callahan, I am on the edge of losing my temper with you and you won't like it when I do. Do not push me."

Cal bit her lip and looked up at him, suddenly, inexplicably, scared. Toby always used the same words— *do not push me*—before his hand shot out, sometimes stopping and sometimes connecting. Sometimes the slap turned into a punch, sometimes a tap; once or twice his palm left finger marks on her cheek. Even worse was when the slap morphed into a caress, into foreplay, into sex she didn't want to have.

Cal bit her bottom lip and tried to get her racing heart under control. Quinn wasn't Toby; he would never, ever hurt her. So then why did she feel like she was being controlled by a bigger, stronger personality than herself?

Oh, God, this had little to do with Toby and everything to do with Quinn and the fact that she'd allowed herself to be vulnerable again. Once again she'd handed over her love, her most precious gift, and once again it had been rejected. Everything she'd worked for—her independence, her sense of self—was slipping away... It felt like *she* was fading away.

She couldn't control the sudden surge of overwhelming anxiety. Feeling like she couldn't get any air, she lifted her hand to her throat and patted her skin, trying to tell herself to breathe. But it was too hot in the club, too noisy and her heart was pounding so hard she felt like it was going to jump out of her chest.

Panic attack. She hadn't had many—she'd started having them in the month before Toby died—but she instantly knew what was happening. Dizziness, a tingling body and ice running through her veins. She wanted to run away from Quinn, this place, her life, but she couldn't. She held onto Quinn's arm, hoping his heat and warmth would pull her back from that dark, horrible place.

"What the—" she heard Quinn's words from a place far away and felt her knees buckling. Then Quinn's arm was around her waist and he pulled her into his embrace, his hand holding her head to his neck, his voice in her ear.

"I've got you, Red. Just breathe. C'mon, baby, just breathe, in and out."

Cal concentrated on his soothing voice, on his strength, on the warmth of his body, his smell. His heat. She pulled in air, slowly, as he suggested, and the ice in her blood melted and the world stopped whirling. She managed to move her arms so she held his hard waist, her hand clutching the fabric of his black button-down shirt. His fingers in her hair massaged her scalp.

"C'mon, Red, get it together. I'm here and you are

fine. You just need to breathe, suck in the disgusting air."

His words caused her to let out a snort of laughter and Quinn's arm around her hips tightened a fraction. "There we go. You're getting there."

Cal pulled in a deep breath, felt her head clearing and nodded, her nose bumping into his jaw.

"If I put you down, will you be able to stand?" Quinn demanded, his lips on her cheek.

"Yeah."

Cal wobbled when her heels hit the floor, but Quinn stabilized her. She stared at the open patch of tanned skin revealed by the collar of his shirt and struggled to make sense of what had just happened. Oh, God, if this wasn't another sign that she had to put some emotional distance between her and Quinn, then she didn't know what was. She couldn't be in a relationship with him, with anybody. If just a couple of words could send her into a tailspin, and his touch could bring her back from the edge, then she needed to get out.

He made her want what she couldn't have, what she wasn't prepared to give. She didn't want to cede that much control over her heart, her thoughts, her life. A relationship meant sacrifice; it meant losing control. It meant bouncing between love and trepidation, between hope and despair.

Love meant being vulnerable.

"Let's get you out of here." Quinn cradled her head between his hands and rested his forehead on hers. She felt his breath, minty fresh, on her cheeks, her nose, whispering across her forehead. "God, Red, what's happening to us?"

Back on the *Red Delicious*, Quinn watched Cal as she carefully sat down on the edge of the sofa's square cushions and stared at the maple floor beneath her feet. They needed to talk, but was she up to it?

He'd always prided himself on being forthright and honest, but this week he'd been anything but. He knew, better than most, how under-the-surface emotions could fester. He'd seen the looks Cal had sent him, the confusion on her face when he made love to her and then emotionally retreated. He was being unfair, but he wasn't sure how to resolve their stalemate.

"I'm going up onto the deck. I need some air."

Quinn nodded and went into the kitchen to pull two wineglasses from the cabinet. He dropped to his haunches and quickly scanned his wine collection before deciding on a robust red. As he reached for the corkscrew, he noticed the thick envelope he'd tossed onto the counter earlier. He'd been so angry with Cal that he hadn't bothered to look inside, but now he was curious. Putting the corkscrew down, he opened the flap and spread the papers on the counter. He sucked in his breath at the photographic documentation of the past few months with Cal.

God, they looked happy, in love, crazy about each other.

There was a photo of him watching her at that art exhibition and he saw love and lust, pride and affection written all over his face. In every photo, the world could see their crazy chemistry, knew their thoughts weren't far away from the bedroom. Some of the photos managed to capture their genuine liking for each other, their trust in each other. He could easily see why the city assumed they were in love.

A camera had flashed in the club earlier, capturing him holding Cal's face in his hands. When that photo appeared online or in tomorrow's social column, they would see a man looking at his woman, adoration on his face.

Because he did adore her—he loved her—but did he love her like *that*? Did he love her enough to walk away from the safety of his lone-wolf lifestyle, enough to give her what she deserved, what she craved? A home, a family—through surrogacy, through adoption, through some nontraditional way—and the love and commitment and fidelity she deserved? Could he put her first, forever and always? Could he build the family he now knew he wanted with her? Could he trust her to put him first, to be the rock he wanted to lean on?

It would be easier to walk away from her right now, tonight, to let whatever they had die a natural death. But if they ended it now, it would take months or years for their friendship to recover, if it ever did. Could he risk that? Could he risk losing her to keep his heart safe?

He didn't know...

Quinn picked up the wine bottle and glasses and took them up to the deck. Cal stood at the railing looking up at the skyscrapers of downtown Vancouver. He loved the deck at night, dark and quiet despite the hectic light show above and behind them.

Cal kicked off her shoes and his eyes traveled along her legs in those tight jeans to her tiny waist, displayed by her snug coat. He put the glasses and wine down and walked toward her, placing his front to her back, pulling aside her hair to place a hot kiss on her elegant neck.

He knew they needed to talk, but he wanted this first, the magic and wonder of her under him. He wasn't sure where they were going, but he needed to love her one more time before words got in the way.

Because words always did.

Early the next morning Cal felt Quinn's kiss on her neck, heard him pull in a deep breath as if he were trying to inhale her. His arm was tight around her; his thigh was flung over hers as if he were trying to hold her in place. It meant nothing, Cal reminded herself; him holding her was a conditioned response.

Cal opened her eyes as Quinn rolled away from her, leaving the bed without speaking to visit the bathroom. She hoped he'd come back to bed, but she didn't really expect him to. Her instinct was proven correct when he walked over to the large window and placed his arm on the glass above his head, his expression disconsolate.

"What caused your panic attack last night?" Quinn asked, without turning around.

Cal didn't bother to pretend that she was asleep. Neither of them had slept and, instead of talking, they'd reached for each other time and time again, as if they knew this conversation would change everything between them. Well, dawn was breaking and the night was over...

Cal pushed back the covers and stood up. She pulled a T-shirt from the pile of laundry on his chair and pulled it over her head. She walked over to the large porthole to stand next to Quinn. He'd pulled on a pair of sleeping shorts and a T-shirt while he was in the bathroom and Cal was grateful. She didn't think they could have this conversation naked.

"You told me you were on the edge of losing your temper," Cal replied, placing her hand on the glass.

She felt Quinn's penetrating look. "And you took that to mean...what? That I would hurt you?"

She lifted a shoulder. "Intellectually, no. Emotionally, I rolled back in time. I have issues about being controlled."

"Because of Carter." Quinn rubbed his hand over his jaw. "But you do know I would never, ever lay a finger on you?"

"I know that, Quinn, I do." Cal looked at him, so big and bold and so very pissed off. "I don't respond well to orders anymore and I didn't like you telling me what to do."

Quinn linked his hands behind his neck, his biceps bulging. "And I had a damn good reason for that. You didn't know what you were walking into last night," Quinn snapped. "FOMO's is, on the surface, a pretty normal club."

"Then why did you have a problem with me going there?" Cal demanded, sitting on the side of the bed, surprised when Quinn sat down next to her, his thigh pressing into hers.

"I said that it's normal on the surface. Girls looking for rich guys, guys looking for pretty girls. I'm on good terms with the bartender, as I am with at least ten others throughout the city, because I pay them to keep an eye on my players, especially the younger ones."

Cal frowned at him. "What? You pay them to spy on your players?"

"I pay them to keep me informed. There are lots of temptations out there for young kids with too much talent and money. Those bartenders and bouncers tell me when they think a player might be in danger of going over the edge. I try to stop it before it gets that far."

"How?"

Quinn looked grim. "Suspension, random drug tests, threats, bribery, coercion. I'm not scared to use what works. I will not let them throw their talent away, throw their future away because they are young and dumb."

"Oh." Cal turned his words over. That was so like Quinn, deeply honorable and innately protective. "Your players were upstairs...so what's upstairs?"

"Strip joint, men and women. Lap dances. Men on men, women on women and any combination thereof. It's a cool place to hang out, to show that you have no issue with your sexuality. I don't care who does what to whom, but the drugs flow through there like water through taps," Quinn stated in a flat voice. "If you had gone up there, on your own, without me, and you were photographed, it would've gone viral."

"I was on my way up there," Cal admitted.

"Yeah, I know. We ducked a bullet. It would've been pretty hard to explain why you were in a strip joint when we are so happily married," Quinn said.

"Except that we are not happily married. Or even properly married."

"No, we're not." Quinn rested his forearms on his thighs, his hands linked. "I looked at the photos, the articles. It seems as if we've done a great job of convincing the public that we are in love."

"But we're not, are we?" Cal asked, her heart in her throat. Well, she might be, but he wasn't.

Quinn pushed an agitated hand through his hair. "It's become complicated, exactly what we didn't want it to be."

He was looking at her as if he expected her to drop another conversational atomic bomb. She could see the trepidation in his eyes, the tension in his hard jaw. He was bracing himself for begging and tears.

She wouldn't do that, Cal decided. She wasn't going

to beg him to love her. She'd rolled that die already and lost. She wasn't going to do it again.

But, God, it hurt. Cal sucked some much needed air and looked for a little bit of courage.

For the first time she made the conscious decision to lie to him. It was, she rationalized, for their greater good.

"I love you. I always have. But I won't let myself be in love with anybody, Quinn, not even you." She couldn't keep sleeping with him, couldn't keep up the pretense. Because she knew with every day she spent with him, every night she slept in his arms, she would fall deeper in love with him and leaving him would become impossible. She needed to save herself and to do that she had to leave. Now.

"Maybe we should—" Cal stopped. She didn't want to say the words because once they were said, she couldn't take them back. Nothing would ever be the same between them again. If she said what she needed to, she'd lose him, lose what little of his love she had. God, she'd had no clue this conversation would be so difficult.

Quinn moved so he sat on his haunches in front of her, his arm on his knee, his fingers encircling her ankle. "Maybe we should stop, Cal. We absolutely should play it safe, be sensible. Sleeping together complicated what was supposed to be a simple arrangement."

And so it starts...

No, don't think about how much it hurts. You can fall

apart later. When you are alone. You've been through worse than this, Callahan. You can cope with a little heartbreak.

Focus on the practicalities. They still had a role to play, a marriage to act out.

"And the press? How do we handle them?"

"We don't do so many public appearances together and when we do, we make sure that we aren't acting so affectionate," Quinn suggested, his voice rough with an emotion she couldn't identify.

Cal tucked her legs under her bottom and pulled his shirt over her knees. "It might be easier if I left...the city, the country."

Besides, being away from him would give her the distance she needed to patch her heart back together.

Shock and denial flashed across his face and Cal lifted a shoulder. "That would be the best option, Quinn. The easiest way to do this."

Quinn muttered a curse and drummed his fingers on his thigh, obviously upset. "Okay, tell me what you're thinking."

"My dad is bored with being idle. He's itching to come back to work and if I give him the smallest excuse, he'll be home in a flash."

"Is he well enough to work?"

"It's been three months so I think so." Cal raked her hair back with her fingers and twisted it into a loose knot at the back of her neck. "And I should get back to my own work. There are problems everywhere that I need to sort out, some I can only fix by being on the ground." Cal nodded as a plan started to form in her head. "I suggest we issue a press statement, saying that I need to return to work, that we're going to do the long-distance marriage thing until I wrap up some projects. Except that the projects take longer than expected and, as a result, we start drifting apart."

Quinn's face gave nothing away and Cal had no idea what he was thinking. Damn, she'd always been able to read him, had always known what he was thinking until recently, when he kept his thoughts hidden from her. She hated it. Despite their best efforts, the last three months had changed their friendship.

They'd chosen the situation; they'd known the risk. Now they had to deal with the fallout.

"That could work," Quinn agreed. "When will you—"

"Go?" Cal finished his sentence. She didn't think she could live with Quinn and not touch him, not make love to him. If she moved anywhere else, then a lot of questions would be asked. The best solution was to leave, as soon as possible.

She just needed to find the courage to walk away, to do what was necessary. For both their sakes.

"ASAP, Quinn. I don't want to draw this out, make it harder than it needs to be." Cal dropped her gaze so he couldn't see how close she was to losing it.

Quinn's arm around her shoulders, him hauling her into his side, told her he'd already noticed. He kissed her temple and rested his head on hers. "We really should've kept this simple, Red."

Cal placed her arm around his neck and closed her eyes, feeling his heat, his hard body and ignoring the throb between her legs, her blood roaring through her veins. "Yeah, we really should've. We weren't very smart, Quinn."

It was the second game of the season and Quinn stood in their newly acquired owners' box in the Mavericks arena looking down at the rink. The seats were starting to fill and there was a buzz in the air.

The fans were excited and he could understand why. Yesterday he, Mac and Kade had signed the final papers giving them a majority ownership of the Mavericks and fulfilling their biggest dream.

Kade and Quinn stood next to him and he saw, and ignored, the long look they exchanged. He took a sip from his coffee cup. He grimaced. The coffee, like everything else over the past month, tasted like crap.

"We are now the official majority owners of the Mavericks," Kade said, a goofy-looking grin on his face. He bumped fists with Mac, who was also wearing a stupid-ass grin. They were still on a high from yesterday, still assimilating the knowledge that the deal was, finally, done.

The Mavericks, as they'd planned ten years ago, was theirs. They'd worked like crazy, taking financial risks, pouring their hearts and souls into the team and it had finally, finally, paid off. Quinn part-owned a professional hockey team, the *only* hockey team.

He should feel happier.

Mac's fist plowed into his shoulder. "I've seen you more excited over a pizza, dude."

Quinn looked across the ice, guilt closing his throat. This was a turning point, a major achievement, and he was sucking the life out of the party. Normally, he'd be the one celebrating the hardest, but little was normal since Cal left.

Everything felt strange, out of place. It was as if his life was now one of those fun-house mirrors, everything distorted, unfocused. But that wasn't his friends' fault; it wasn't anyone's fault but his. He made his choices and was living with the very crappy consequences.

Suck it up, Rayne. He dragged a smile onto his face and lifted his cup in a salute. "Here's to us. We kicked ass."

Kade's small smile acknowledged Quinn's effort to get into the swing of things. "Good try, but your level of enthusiasm still sucks. So, let's talk about it."

"Might as well," Mac agreed.

Oh, God. What was with his friends and their desire to talk things through? They were guys. Guys didn't talk stuff to death.

"Nothing to talk about," Quinn snapped and frowned at Mac. "And we need to get down to the locker room."

"We have time," Mac replied.

Kade removed a stick of gum from his pocket, unwrapped the paper, keeping his eyes on Quinn. "Nothing to talk about? Really? Except Callahan, that is. How is she?"

So it looked like they were going to discuss Quinn's absent wife and his nonmarriage. "She arrived safely in Lesotho. I haven't spoken to her recently."

"Why not?" Kade asked.

"She's in a mountainous region with a bad signal," Quinn snapped.

"Wren manages to talk to her every couple of days, so do Brodie and Rory," Mac commented, his face and tone bland.

Busted. How could he worm his way out of this? What excuse could he use? Quinn rubbed his temple and decided he was too tired to look for one. Besides, these were his best friends, his safety net.

"It's just easier not to talk to her." Quinn took another sip of coffee and grimaced. He placed the mug on a high table and pushed it away.

"You miss her."

Miss her? That was such a stupid, tame, word for what he felt. He couldn't sleep, couldn't concentrate, couldn't think for missing her.

He absolutely missed his lover, missed his friend. "Yeah, I miss her."

"Why did she leave again?" Mac asked.

Quinn rubbed the back of his neck. "We decided that the...situation was getting out of control."

"Out of control how?"

Kade looked at Mac; Mac shook his head and echoed Kade's look of confusion. Really, was Quinn going to have to draw them a picture? "Neither of us wanted a happily-ever-after deal. Neither of us wanted to commit so we dialed it down before we…before we found ourselves doing that."

Kade tried to contain his mirth, but Mac just let it rip, his laughter rumbling over them. Quinn felt his fist clench and wondered if he would be forgiven for punching his best friend shortly after they realized their biggest professional and business triumph. And before a game.

Probably not.

"Glad that I amuse you. Moving the hell on—"

"How can you not realize that you and Cal are in a committed relationship, that you have been for years?" Kade asked, bemused.

"What are you talking about?" Quinn demanded.

"Moron, you've been friends for twenty years. That's commitment right there. Easy, natural, something that just is."

He'd try to keep this simple and maybe they'd understand. "Yeah, we were committed to a friendship, not a love affair."

"You worked to keep your friendship alive. You wanted to keep that connection. It was very damn important to you. And to her. You've been more committed to each other than anybody else in your lives. Your commitment to each other is longer than our friendship, longer than your career with the Mavericks, so much more meaningful than your relationship with your family. And you're both wusses, running away from each other," Mac bluntly said.

Oh…hell. Quinn wanted to deny his words, wanted to argue, but he couldn't find anything to say. There were reasons why he couldn't have a be-mine relationship with Cal.

"It's not as simple as that," Quinn croaked the words out.

Two sets of eyebrows lifted. God, he'd never felt so exposed, so completely vulnerable. How could he tell them, these two masculine, *virile* men…

He rubbed his temple and when he looked up at them, his eyes reflected his anguish. "Cal wants kids. I can't give her any."

Kade and Mac stared at him for a long time and while he saw sympathy on their faces, he didn't see pity. Thank God. If he had, he would've handed in his man card. Kade tapped his fingers on the table, a sure sign that he was thinking. "Why do you think that?"

Quinn explained and they listened intently. Kade frowned and shook his head. "You need to get a second opinion. I don't think you can rely on one blood test years ago as a definitive diagnosis."

Mac nodded. "And, if it turns out you can't have kids, then there are other options. Adoption, surrogacy, sperm banks. Hell, I'll even donate some of my magnificent boys to the cause."

Kade choked on his beer and Quinn's mouth dropped open. Then humor—unexpected but welcome—bubbled to the surface. He shook his head. "It's bad enough working with you, training you—having to raise a mini-you would do my head in."

"The point is, there are options. But—" Kade sent him a hard, cool, assessing look "—before you get there you have to decide whether you want Cal in your life or not. Separate and apart from the giving-her-kids issue."

"Which he does," Mac interjected.

Which Quinn did. More than he wanted to keep working, coaching, *breathing*. His life without her in it had no meaning, no color, absolutely no direction. And even less joy. Kade was right: he'd never been able to commit to anyone because he'd always—even if it was only on a subconscious level—been committed to Callahan. He loved her. He'd always loved her. His subconscious knew what it wanted and it had been waiting a damn long time for his body and his brain to catch up.

"Yep, he's getting there." Mac gripped Quinn's shoulder, their equivalent of a girly hug.

Quinn felt he should say something, should express his gratitude that he had these two guys solidly in his corner. But hell, what could he say that didn't make him sound like he'd grown a pair of ovaries?

"Thanks," he eventually muttered.

Mac grinned. "Well, you know that we'd take a bullet for you. Not in the head, or in the heart, but maybe like in the ass...or the big toe."

Quinn, for the first time that night, for the first time in a month, laughed. As his laughter rumbled out, he felt his mobile vibrate. He pulled it out and swiped the screen with his thumb.

His laughter died and something that felt like hope took its place. "I need to go."

Mac snatched the mobile from his hand, read the message and handed the phone to Kade. Quinn was too shocked to object to them reading his messages. All he cared about was going home.

Kade slapped the phone back into Quinn's hand.

"I have to do this," he said, hoping they'd understand. "Cal and I need to talk."

Neither Mac nor Kade said anything for a while and Quinn's heart sank. He understood their reluctance, he was, after, running out on his responsibilities. The Mavericks, the game…they were important, sure, but Cal was his *life*.

Then they grinned and he knew that they'd been messing with him. Jerks.

"Go, we'll handle your responsibilities here," Kade told him. He grinned. "I mean, really, how difficult can coaching be?"

Quinn shoved a hand through his hair and narrowed his eyes at Kade. At the door he turned and sent Kade a withering glare. "Payback is a bitch, Webb."

Kade just laughed. "Get the hell out of here, Rayne, before we change our minds."

Quinn bolted.

Eleven

Living her life without Quinn was like trying to make the world spin in another direction. It simply didn't work. It made her feel dizzy and ditzy and…sad. Bereft. Alone.

She'd tried. She'd given it her best shot and, after a month, she was over living on the other side of the world, trying to remember why it was better that she and Quinn were apart. The only thing that was true, real, important was that they stay linked, that he remain a part of her life, in any way she could get him.

She didn't know how that would work, what role she was going to play, but they could work it out. They *would* work it out. He'd been the biggest part of her life for most of her life, the person she'd loved best all these years, and while she loved him, fiercely, she'd take him any way she could get him.

Cal opened the door to Quinn's home and dropped her overnight bag to the floor. Although she knew Quinn would be at the arena, preparing for a Mavericks game, she tipped her head, listening for movement, hoping she'd hear him upstairs. Hoping she could see him, drink him in.

Cal played with her cell phone as she walked toward the huge windows. She placed her shoulder against the glass and stared out at the water; she'd missed this view, missed his home.

Missed him with every atom of her being.

She'd always thought that love was something ethereal, an emotion that made you happier, prettier, smarter, more worthwhile. She'd dived into a marriage with Toby in order to feel safe and protected, in the hope that he'd take her to a place where grief didn't exist, where nothing could hurt her. She'd miscalculated there. Toby had hurt her and she'd been slapped in the face with everything she'd been running from.

His death had released her and, instead of trying to work through her issues with men, commitment and marriage, she'd dismissed both the species and the tradition, choosing to go it alone.

Only to find all she wanted and needed in the man who'd always been her rock, who made her laugh, who'd always encouraged her to fly but who would catch her if she crashed.

Because love wasn't perfection. It wasn't big houses and gourmet meals, designer clothes and fake smiles. Love wasn't the storybook kiss in the rain. It wasn't red roses or deep, soulful conversations.

Love was messy. Love was imperfect. Love was sarcastic text messages and two-minute phone calls, buying takeout and eating it on the bed before making love. Love was arguing and sharing the shower, stealing his cup of coffee when you were running out the door, morning kisses before teeth were brushed. Love was a friendship set on fire. Love was not running when things got tough; it was having the courage to reach out for more.

Love was traveling across an ocean from one continent to another to tell her best friend, the man she loved best, that she wanted everything he could give her, whether that was a little or a lot.

Cal took a deep breath, felt her heart kick up. She couldn't call him. He was preparing for a game and he wouldn't answer. Quinn had tunnel vision when he was in the zone and he was never more in the zone than when he was preparing for a Mavericks game. But she could send him a text. He'd get it when the game was over and that would give her some time to think about what to say to him.

For the first time ever, she couldn't find her words with Quinn, couldn't explain what she was thinking and feeling. Maybe it was because this time the words she needed to say were too important, the feelings too scary. She typed and erased four messages and cursed herself.

Keep it simple.

Hi, I wanted to tell you that I miss you, that I miss us. Maybe you can give me a call and we can chat about us, our marriage? Please?

Cal pushed the send button on her phone and bit her bottom lip. What if he didn't reply? What if he came home and was upset to see her back? Oh, God, what if he'd moved on? What if he came home with a puck-bunny groupie on his arm?

Maybe coming back to Vancouver was a bad move, she thought, staring at the ocean, fighting back her tears. Maybe she should leave. Go back to Africa and then onto India, bury herself in her work.

Except she'd done that, had tried to push him away, had tried to forget him, but she'd failed spectacularly. No, she wouldn't run. She'd wait, talk to him, repair whatever she could of their friendship.

She realized that he would never love her, not the way she wanted him to, but they could be friends and maybe that would be enough.

So she'd stay here and wait.

Thank God he was one of the bosses because blowing off an important game, leaving the stadium before his team was about to go on the ice, would get his ass canned if he were an employee, Quinn thought as he swung his Ducati in and out of traffic. As soon as he got to the yacht, he'd call Cal back, find out where she was. Then he'd call the team's pilot and tell him to file a flight plan for their company jet.

He needed to grab some gear and his passport— God, he couldn't forget his passport. Quinn steered his bike into his parking spot at the marina, ripped off his helmet, shoved it under his arm and started jogging toward the access gate and the *Red Delicious*. As he ran, he looked down at his cell, his thumb hovering over the green button to call Cal back. What would he say? How could he express everything that was in his heart?

Why did this have to be so damn difficult? He didn't want to spill his soul on a telephone or via an internet connection. Nope, if he was going to make an idiot of himself, then he was going do it properly, face-to-face.

And if that meant flying halfway around the world, then that was what he would do. Besides, he knew he could persuade her to his way of thinking—a proper marriage, love, staying together, being together—by kissing her, helping her get naked. Hey, a guy had to use whatever worked.

Quinn stormed onto the yacht, belted up the stairs and whipped open the door. He threw his helmet onto the chair at the door and thundered down the stairs to his cabin. He pushed the green button and the call rang as he yanked open the door to his walk-in closet. Stepping inside he grabbed some T-shirts and tucked them under his arm.

One ring, two, three, four—God, she had to answer.

He tossed the shirts onto his bed and dropped to his haunches next to his nightstand. He stared at the small wall safe in the table and couldn't remember the code. What if she didn't answer? What if he couldn't get ahold of her? What would he do? Where would he go?

"Hello?"

Quinn stood up abruptly, swore and rubbed the back of his neck. "Hi, sorry. I didn't think you were going to answer." He spat the words out, hardly able to hear his own voice above the thundering of his heart.

"Hi. Shouldn't you be at the game?"

"I should. I'm not." Just hearing her voice made sense. *She made sense.* "Where are you?"

"Why?"

"Because wherever you are, I'm on my way there." God, he sounded like an idiot. "I mean, I'll get there. Give me some time. You're right—we need to talk."

"You're coming to me?"

He thought he heard amusement in her voice but dismissed it as a figment of his imagination. It wasn't like he was thinking straight at the moment. "Yeah, the company jet is at my disposal. It'll get me where I need to go. So, can you text me directions?"

"I can do that. But it's pretty simple, I can tell you over the phone."

"God, Red, I can't think straight, and I definitely won't remember anything you say. Just text me. I'll get to wherever I need to be as soon as I can." And he prayed it wouldn't take more than a day or two.

"Okay, um, great. See you soon." Cal disconnected and Quinn stared at his blank screen, a frown on his face. Dammit, that was it? That was all she had for him? He was flying out to see a woman he loved and all she could say was *see you soon*? God, she was the most infuriating, crazy, annoying brat he'd ever laid eyes on. The only woman he'd ever loved, would ever love.

And, yeah, two days was better than two weeks, two months, two years, never. So he'd be a man and suck it up...

His phone flashed and Quinn swiped his thumb across the screen. He read the message, frowned and read it again.

At your bedroom door, turn right. Walk up the stairs and look for the girl holding the bottle of wine and two glasses.

Holy, holy, *holy* crap.

Quinn thundered back up the stairs, skidded into the lounge and stopped by the cream-colored sofa, his hands gripping its back with white-knuckled fingers. Cal noticed that his chest was heaving and his breathing was erratic. She was amazed, thrilled, that her presence could raise the heartbeat of this superfit man.

Her man. Maybe...

She looked for something to say, some witty comment to break their charged silence, something to slice through the tension. She had nothing so she lifted her half-full glass of wine. "Want some?"

"Wine? No." Quinn's voice, deep and dark, rumbled across her skin as he walked toward her, his eyes a little wild and a lot determined. Her throat closed up as he narrowed the distance between them and she allowed him to pull the glass from her hand, watching as he placed it on the coffee table in front of her. "That's not what I want."

"What do you want?" Cal asked, tipping her head back to look at him, wishing he would touch her, kiss her.

"You. Any damn way I can get you." Quinn's gaze dropped from her eyes to her mouth, where he lingered as if he was fighting the urge to kiss her. Cal sighed when his hand cupped her shoulder, skimmed up her throat, her jaw, stopping when his palm rested on her cheek, his fingers in her hair.

Cal needed to touch him so she placed her hand on his chest. "Your heart is racing," she murmured.

The corners of Quinn's mouth kicked up. "Yeah, it started doing that when I saw your name on my screen and it went into overdrive when I realized you are here, in my home, and not a continent away. Why are you here, Cal?"

She tried to tell him why, but the words wouldn't come. Instead of telling him that she loved him, that she wanted a lifetime with him, she bit her lip.

"Why were you going to hijack the company jet to come to me?" she whispered, hoping he was braver than her.

"I was going to fly over there and beg you to come home. To me." Quinn's voice was saturated with emotion. "My life…is not that exciting anymore. Not without you in it."

She needed clarity, needed to know what he meant by that statement. "As a friend? As a lover?"

"As my everything," Quinn whispered the words against her lips and the last, tiny kernel of fear dissolved. "You're the only woman I've ever loved, the only person I fully trust."

"Quinn." Cal bunched the fabric of his shirt in her hand, closing her eyes when his lips touched her temple, her cheekbone, the lids of her eyes.

"Nothing gives me as much of a thrill as I get when I wake up with you in my arms, when I come home and you're here. Nothing gets my heart racing like making love to you. Nothing feels as good as watching you shatter when I'm inside you. You are my highest peak, my biggest wave, my fastest ride."

Cal linked her arms around his neck and stood on her tiptoes to brush her lips against his mouth, to push her breasts into his chest, her hips into his. If she could climb inside him, she would. "Quinn."

Quinn kissed her and she felt his love in his lips, in the way he tasted her. His lips sipped at her; his tongue traced the fullness of her bottom lip, the edges of her teeth, before it slid inside to tangle with her tongue. It was a kiss that promised, that soothed, that excited. It told the story of their past and painted a picture for the future, of a friendship set on fire.

Then his kiss slowed, he hesitated and pulled back to look at her, a question in his eyes.

"Why did you come back?" he asked, his hands on her hips, the tips of his fingers digging into her skin. Cal touched his cheek and realized there was doubt in his eyes, and fear. Fear that he was the only one feeling this way...

Cal swallowed, humbled by the fact that this strong, brave man was insecure, that he needed her reassurance, that he wasn't the only one who was risking his heart. "I came home because you are, simply, my home. You have always been my deepest connection, my best friend. You bring out the best in me. You make me want to be better, do better."

Quinn's eyes softened, turned a brighter green. "Are we saying that we love each other?"

Cal nodded her agreement but didn't drop her eyes from his. He just looked at her, waiting for her to verbalize her thoughts, to make them real. "I do love you." But she'd always loved him, so she thought clarity was needed. "I am so *in love* with you."

"As I am with you," Quinn replied, resting his temple against the top of her head, hugging her to him. "God, baby, I've missed you so much."

"I've missed you too. I never knew how long nights

could be without you beside me," Cal said, snuggling in as her tension drained away. "I didn't think you could love me, but I knew I had to be near you, if only as a friend."

Quinn's hand squeezed her butt in a way that was anything but friendly. "Like we could be in the same room without wanting to get each other naked. Talking about getting naked…"

"Were we? I thought we were going to spend the next couple of hours being all mushy," Cal teased him, not quite able to imagine her adrenaline-seeking man being ridiculously romantic.

"I do my best romancing naked," Quinn assured her, his hand tugging on the hem of her flowing, rust-colored sweater.

Cal lifted her arms and he pulled the sweater over her head and tossed it to the floor. Instead of reaching for her, Quinn held her away from him, his face questioning. "Is that what you need from me, romance?"

Cal cocked her head. "Would you give it to me?"

"I will try to give you whatever you need to make you happy. Fidelity, respect, love—that's a given. I'm not a romantic guy, but if that's what you need to feel secure, I'll try."

His sincerity hit her in the gut and her jumpy heart settled, sighed. "I don't need the gestures of romance, Quinn. I just need you. The Quinn I've always known is the Quinn I want in my life. I just need you to tell me you love me occasionally and to get me naked as often as possible, and I'm grand."

"I have no problem with telling you I love you. I always have and it seems to be as natural as breathing."

"Me too."

Sadness dimmed the happiness in his eyes. "What about kids, Cal? I can't give you kids."

Cal hastened to assure him that her love wasn't conditional. "I'm still not convinced about that, but we'll work it out. You and I, we can work anything out, as long as we do it together."

Cal's eyes drank him in. His beautiful eyes, his jaw rough with stubble, his relaxed mouth. His hair was longer and not so spiky and...

Cal laughed and she lifted her hand to a spot just above his ear.

Quinn raised an eyebrow. "What?"

Cal tugged the white feather out of his hair and held it up for him to see. "I think my mom approves."

Quinn touched the feather with his index finger before pulling Cal into his arms and dropping his face into her neck. "I do love you, Red."

Cal felt his heart thudding under her hand and knew her happy-ever-after had arrived. Their life together, she decided, was going to be an amazing ride.

Epilogue

Three months later...

"Now tell me this wasn't a grand idea," Mac demanded, lifting a champagne bottle to refresh Brodie's and Rory's champagne flutes. The six of them, with Rosie and Cody, were sitting on the veranda, having just come back to the luxury house after an afternoon spent on the beach.

Cal had no problem telling Mac that his impetuous decision that they spend a week at the house they jointly owned in Puerto Rico was a fine idea and she lifted her untouched glass in his direction. "Fantastic idea, Mac."

"Wait until you live through a hurricane here," Rory muttered, but her eyes laughed at her husband.

Mac took his toddler daughter from Rory and dropped a kiss on her puckered lips. "It was just a little wind, Rorks, and you took shelter in my big, brawny arms."

"Well, one arm. The other was fairly useless at the time," Rory corrected him. "God, you were a terrible patient."

Their friends laughed when Mac scowled at her. Cal leaned back in her chair and picked her feet up to tuck her heels on the edge of the chair, thinking that it wouldn't be long before she wouldn't be able to sit like this. She was surprised Quinn hadn't noticed her rounder shape.

For the last day or so, since they'd left Vancouver, she'd been wondering how to tell him he was going to be a dad, probably in around thirty weeks or so. He'd be surprised and, she hoped, ecstatically happy. Even happier than they presently were…if that was even possible.

Quinn, sitting next to Kade, picked up Cody's foot and bent his head to gently nibble the baby's arch, causing Cody to chuckle heartily every time. They'd been playing this game for ten minutes and neither of them was bored with it yet. Cal felt her eyes fill with tears and after she'd blinked them away, she caught Kade's gaze and saw him tip his head, his eyes quizzical.

Kade always seemed to sense a secret just as it was ready to be divulged. And what was she waiting for? These were Quinn's best friends—her best friends—their family. Quinn wouldn't care how he heard that he was going to be a dad, and they'd get a kick out of seeing his happiness.

Cal flicked her eyes to Cody, gave Kade the tiniest nod and his eyes flashed with understanding and joy.

"Quinn—" she started to speak, but her words drained away. She bit her lip, her mind a blank. It was such good news, crazy-good news, but her throat had closed from too much emotion.

"Hey, butthead—" Kade jumped into her silence, winking at Cal "—did you ever go back to the doctor to redo those fertility tests?"

Quinn looked up at him and scowled. "I'm playing a rather excellent game with your son and you have to spoil the moment by raising *that* subject? Thanks, Webb."

Kade wasn't remotely chastised. "Well, did you?"

Quinn reached out and took Cal's hand in his and she felt the tension in his fingers. "Cal and I decided that we'd do it when the season ended, when we had a moment to breathe. We're taking a little time for ourselves before we go down that road."

"But you do want kids?" Kade demanded.

Cal saw Quinn's Adam's apple bob and the slow, definite nod of his head. "I want whatever we can have. As long as Cal is at the center of our family, I'm good."

Tears, silent and powerful, rolled down Cal's face. Her small sob had Quinn whipping his head around to look at her and his eyes widened in shock. "Crap! What did I say? Red, don't cry—jeez! I'm sorry, I know it's a sensitive subject and Kade is a moron for bringing it up."

"I agree with that," Mac chimed in.

Cal let out a laugh and placed her hand on Quinn's cheek, pulling his frowning face back to hers. "Stop looking at Kade like you want to thump him, darling. He's actually being a good guy, trying to help me out here."

"Told you so," Kade said with a smirk, rubbing his unshaven chin across Cody's fuzzy head.

Quinn frowned. "What do you mean?"

Cal blinked away her tears and smiled. She reached past Quinn and tapped Cody's foot. "We're going to have one of these." She looked at Rosie, who was dipping her fingers into Mac's beer glass and shoving her wet digits into her mouth. "Or maybe a pink one, like Rosie. Um…maybe you should move your beer glass out of your daughter's reach, Mac."

Mac picked up his drink and Rosie let out a yell of protest.

Rory covered her eyes with her hand. "Oh, God, she's definitely a Maverick. Heaven help me."

Quinn shook his head, still confused. "I don't understand. What are you trying to say, Red?"

Cal smiled and pulled his hand to her stomach. "Do you remember I asked you for some of your boys?"

He was still confused. "Yeah, and I told you that I don't have any."

Cal laughed. "Four pregnancy tests and a scan the

day before yesterday says you do, my darling. So, do you want to come on an adventure with me, Q? You, me and our munchkin?"

Quinn lowered his forehead to hers, his eyes glistening with hope, excitement and undiluted joy. "Red, I love you to distraction and you should know by now that I would go anywhere with you. You, and them—" he jerked a thumb toward his friends "—are my family, but I'm thrilled, ecstatic, that we're making it bigger."

"We're halfway to having our own junior Mavericks team, men," Mac drawled. "Another from each of us and we can put a team on the ice. But, really, to make an impact, we'd need a couple more…"

* * * * *

#2491 THE TYCOON'S SECRET CHILD
Texas Cattleman's Club: Blackmail • by Maureen Child
When CEO Wesley Jackson's Twitter account is hacked, it's to reveal that he has a secret daughter! Amidst scandal, he tracks down his old fling, but can he convince her he's truly ready to be a father—and a husband?

#2492 ONE BABY, TWO SECRETS
Billionaires and Babies • by Barbara Dunlop
Wallflower Kate Dunhem goes undercover as a wild child to save her infant niece, but a torrid affair with a stranger who has his own secrets may turn her world upside down...

#2493 THE RANCHER'S NANNY BARGAIN
Callahan's Clan • by Sara Orwig
Millionaire Cade Callahan needs a nanny for his baby girl, but hiring his best friend's gorgeous, untouchable sister might have been a mistake! Especially once he can no longer deny the heat between them...

#2494 AN HEIR FOR THE TEXAN
Texas Extreme • by Kristi Gold
Years after a family feud ended their romance, wealthy rancher Austin reunites with his ex. Their chemistry is still just as explosive! But what will he do when he learns she's been withholding a serious secret?

#2495 SINGLE MOM, BILLIONAIRE BOSS
Billionaire Brothers Club • by Sheri WhiteFeather
Single mother Meagan Quinn has paid a price for her past mistakes, but when her sexy billionaire boss gives her a second chance, is she walking into a trap...or into a new life—with him?

#2496 THE BEST MAN'S BABY
by Karen Booth
She's the maid of honor. Her ex is the best man. Their friend's wedding must go off without a hitch—no fighting, no scandals, no hooking up! But after just one night, she's pregnant and the baby *might* be his...

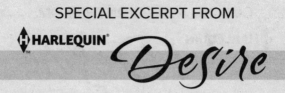
"Look where your dallying has gotten you," the email
read.

"What the hell?" There was an attachment, and even
though Wes had a bad feeling about all of this, he opened
it. The photograph popped onto his computer screen.

Staring down at the screen, his gaze locked on the
image of the little girl staring back at him. "What the—"

She looked just like him.

Panic and fury tangled up inside him and tightened
into a knot that made him feel like he was choking.

A daughter? He had a child. Judging by the picture
she looked to be four or five years old, so unless it was
an old photo, there was only one woman who could be
the girl's mother. And just like that, the woman was back
front and center in his mind.

How the hell had this happened? Stupid. He knew how
it had happened. What he didn't know was why he hadn't

been told. Wes rubbed one hand along the back of his neck. Still staring at the smiling girl on the screen, he opened a new window and went to Twitter.

Somebody had hacked his account. His new account name was, as promised in the email, Deadbeatdad. If he didn't get this stopped fast, it would go viral and might start interfering with his business.

Instantly, Wes made some calls and turned the mess over to his IT guys to figure out. Meanwhile, he was too late to stop #Deadbeatdad from spreading. The Twitterverse was already moving on it. Now he had a child to find and a reputation to repair. Snatching up the phone, he stabbed the button for his assistant's desk. "Robin," he snapped. "Get Mike from PR in here now."

He didn't even wait to hear her response, just slammed the phone down and went back to his computer. He brought up the image of the little girl—his daughter—again and stared at her. What was her name? Where did she live?

Then thoughts of the woman who had to be the girl's mother settled into his brain. Isabelle Gray. She'd disappeared from his life years ago—apparently with his child.

Jaw tight, eyes narrowed, Wes promised himself he was going to get to the bottom of all of this.

Don't miss
THE TYCOON'S SECRET CHILD
by USA TODAY *bestselling author Maureen Child,*
available now wherever
Harlequin® Desire books and ebooks are sold.

www.Harlequin.com

Whatever You're Into... Passionate Reads

Looking for more passionate reads from Harlequin®?
Fear not! Harlequin® Presents, Harlequin® Desire and
Harlequin® Blaze offer you irresistible romance stories
featuring powerful heroes.

♦HARLEQUIN *Presents.*

Do you want alpha males, decadent glamour and jet-set
lifestyles? Step into the sensational, sophisticated world of
Harlequin® Presents, where sinfully tempting heroes ignite a
fierce and wickedly irresistible passion!

♦HARLEQUIN *Desire*

Harlequin® Desire novels are powerful, passionate and
provocative contemporary romances set against a backdrop of
wealth, privilege and sweeping family saga. Alpha heroes with
a soft side meet strong-willed but vulnerable heroines amid a
dramatic world of divided loyalties, high-stakes conflict and
intense emotion.

♦HARLEQUIN *Blaze*

Harlequin® Blaze stories sizzle with strong heroines and
irresistible heroes playing the game of modern love and lust.
They're fun, sexy and always steamy.

Be sure to check out our full selection of books
within each series every month!

HPASSION.